Taming BULL

INTERNATIONAL BESTSELLING AUTHOR
HARLEY STONE

COPYRIGHT

Copyright © 2020 by Harley Stone
All rights reserved.
Published in the United States

This book contains material protected under International and Federal Copyright Laws and Treaties. Any unauthorized reprint or use of this material is prohibited. No part of this book may be reproduced or transmitted in any form or by any means, electronic or mechanical, including photocopying, recording, or by any information storage and retrieval system without express written permission from the authors, except in the case of brief quotations embodied in critical articles and reviews.

Taming Bull is a work of fiction. Names, characters, places, and incidents are the products of the author's imagination and are used fictitiously. Any resemblance to actual events, locales, or persons, living or dead, is entirely coincidental.

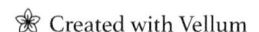

❀ Created with Vellum

*This one's for the readers who never let me give up.
You know who you are.
Thank you!*

PROLOGUE

Lily

MY COMMON SENSE rebelled the instant I sat in the passenger's seat of the shiny black Jag. My fight or flight instincts cranked up to a hundred and I forced myself to focus on breathing, not reaching for the handle to hurl myself out of the car. I was in danger, and I'd survived this long by hiding. Now, I'd agreed to testify against my attacker, drawing a gigantic target on my forehead. What the hell was I thinking? Sure, a motorcycle club of military veterans had offered me their protection—which was why I'd agreed to this insanity in the first place—but I didn't know them and could easily be taking a luxurious drive from the proverbial frying pan into the fire.

At least I'd arrive in style. Wearing baggy sweats, a T-shirt, and worn old sneakers, I settled into the Jag's plush interior and buckled my seatbelt as thoughts continued to race through my mind. There'd be a trial. I'd have to testify. *He'd* be there, watching as I told the world what he'd done to me.

Emily, the well-dressed, confident lawyer who'd talked me into coming out of hiding to confront the bastard, slid behind the wheel and gave me a bolstering smile. "You're doing the right thing, Lily. Havoc is a good guy, and he doesn't deserve to be locked up for helping you."

Emily was phenomenal at her job. She'd balanced out the guilt and fear, making it sound like she stood firmly in camp Lily and her priority was to keep me safe and seek justice for my attacker. But she was being paid to be team Havoc. I needed to keep that in mind during all her talks and make sure her loyalty to her employers didn't leave my broke ass hanging out in the cold.

Havoc.

Thoughts of my rescuer invaded. Until Emily showed up on the doorstep of the shelter I'd been staying at with her song and dance, I didn't even think my rescuer was human. The night of the attack, he looked like an avenging angel, cloaked in shadow, his eyes glowing with fire and fury as he ripped my attacker off me, flung him to the side, and then proceeded to beat the shit out of him.

But it turned out Havoc was human after all. Human and in jail for attempted murder. He'd played the role of good Samaritan and proven the old adage that no good deed goes unpunished. I couldn't let him rot in jail for helping me, not when it was within my power to help him. Not when the world had such a shortage on good guys.

Emily parked in front of an old fire station and faced me. "You're very brave for doing this."

I didn't feel brave; I felt backed into a corner. If I didn't stand up for the man who'd helped me, I'd never be able to look myself in the mirror again. I was still figuring out this fucked up mess called life and there weren't many rules I followed, but I'd seen karma work itself out enough to fear its backlash. I wasn't acting out of bravery, but rather cowardice. My life already sucked ass. I didn't need karma out to get me.

I grabbed my bags from the backseat and followed Emily into the old fire station. A blond biker named Wasp joined us at the door. "This all you brought with you?" he asked, eyeing the duffle bag in my hand and the backpack slung over my shoulder.

This was all I had in the entire world. I had no idea how long I'd have to stay with the Dead Presidents, and anything left behind at the shelter would have disappeared before I returned. And it's not like I was rolling in resources to replace my shit. "Yeah. This is it."

Wasp held out a hand. "Hand it over. I'll carry it up for you."

He didn't come across as the thieving type, but I liked to keep my stuff close. Tightening my grip on my bags, I replied, "Thanks, but I got it."

He shrugged and followed us. A few bikers were milling about, and they greeted us as we marched through a huge open area full of sofas and televisions to a staircase. On the second floor, Wasp pointed out the women's locker style restroom before leading me to a door. "I'm gonna put you up next door to Candice," he said.

I had no idea who Candice was, but before I could ask, Wasp opened a door and gestured us inside. Then he knocked on the next door.

"You're staying here tonight, right?" I asked Emily, mentally cursing the slight quaver in my voice, as she swept me into the room. The small space offered a queen-sized bed, a dresser, and a small closet. It was clean and warm, and I'd be comfortable here as soon as Emily reassured me she wasn't about to lock me in and abandon me.

"Yes. I'll be on the third floor."

"Promise you won't leave?"

She met my gaze. "I have to leave to get an overnight bag, but I'll be back. Let's exchange numbers so you can find me if you need me."

Emily's phone was some high-tech looking device with a cute protective case. Mine was a dented old piece of shit I had on a prepaid plan in case my boss needed to get in touch with me to work extra shifts. As a part-time employee struggling to keep my phone on and my belly full, I needed all the hours I could get.

My phone chimed with her incoming text, and I saved her contact information as I wandered over and sat on the bed. The mattress was firm, but comfortable, a huge improvement to the shelter's bunk bed I'd been tossing and turning on for the past few nights.

Wasp entered with another short brunette and a dog. "Emily, Lily, this is Candice." Facing the brunette, he added, "Emily's the lawyer I told you about. She'll probably need to get with you soon and take your statement."

"Okay." The brunette smiled. "Whenever you're ready. Not like I have a lot going on right now."

Emily looked confused. "Wasp and I need to talk, and I need to grab my overnight bag. I'll check on you both when I get back." She hooked her arm in Wasp's and towed him toward the door.

Before I could respond, they were out the door. Just like that, she left me. In a place full of big scary bikers, no less. My heart started racing and it felt like the room was closing in on me. The dog walked right in and put his head on my lap, staring up at me like I was the most important person he'd ever met.

"That's Boots." Candice followed the dog and patted his back. "He's pretty much the best guy on the planet."

Boots appeared to be some sort of German shepherd mix, grey with spots of black and white. "Does the door lock?" I blurted out.

Candice watched me like I might grab the dog and run, which, I was considering. "Yeah. The key's on the dresser." She pointed and I looked and confirmed she was right.

My pulse slowed as I absently stroked Boots's fur and watched Candice, wondering what her deal was. "Do you live here? With the bikers?"

She shook her head. "No. Noah Kinlan attacked me, too. I'm here to testify, just like you."

Ah. She was one of the "others" Emily had mentioned. "When?" I asked.

She gave me a blank look. "The trial starts in a few days, but I'm not sure when I'll be called to testify."

Shaking my head, I tried again. "No. When did he attack you?"

"A few years ago."

"Did you know him?"

"No. I was going to U-dub, and he attacked me on my way to class. I'd seen him around campus, but I didn't know him."

I'd been on my way home from work when Noah had grabbed me. I didn't even see him. "Did you report it?" The question came out packed with anger and indignation, sounding a lot like an accusation. For the life of me, I didn't know why. Candice was a victim. I shouldn't be upset with her, but I was. If she was attacked years ago, it was her duty to report it and put the bastard behind bars. He never would have gotten to me if she'd done her duty.

"Yes. Actually, I did." She pulled herself up to the full height of her five-foot nothing frame and stared me down. Short and thin, with brown hair that fell past her shoulders, we looked like we could be related. Were we Noah's type? Did he have other victims out there who looked like us? "Well, I tried, at least." She visibly wilted and puffed out a breath. "People came after me. Lawyers. Associates. Reporters. Friends of the Mayor. They threatened, and I was stressed and scared. My grades started slipping and a couple of the professors singled me out. I lost a big scholarship for a bullshit reason and had to drop out. Yeah, I reported him, and it cost me my degree. Did you report him?"

My stomach bottomed out as I realized I wasn't so much angry with Candice, but at myself. "No. I..." I ran. I hid. I hadn't even thought of the women Noah would attack after me.

I'm a fucking hypocrite.

Her expression softened. "It's okay. Probably wouldn't have mattered anyway." When her gaze met mine again, there was steel and determination behind it. "But now, it's different. We're gonna take this fucker down, and make sure he doesn't hurt anyone ever again."

Now that was a plan I could get behind. I nodded, feeling emboldened by the conviction in her voice. Maybe we could win a fight against the mayor's son after all. And if not, it wasn't like I had anything to lose. I had no college scholarships or family at risk. Hell, I didn't even have a car or a permanent residence. I barely had a job.

"I should probably go and let you get settled. There's a huge fully stocked kitchen downstairs if you get hungry or thirsty. I'm right next door if you have any questions or need anything." Candice walked toward the door. Her gaze snagged on the dog still staring at me like I hung the moon, the stars, and all his treats, and I half expected her to call him away. Instead, she leveled a stern look at him. "Boots, watch over Lily."

"Thank you," I said, more relieved than I would care to admit. There was something about dogs that takes away the lonely and makes a person feel protected and loved. I needed that now. Desperately.

She nodded. "The Dead Presidents are good guys. You're safe here."

Safe.

The word bounced around in my head like some foreign language I couldn't quite grasp. 'Safe' could have easily been a territory on Jupiter for all I knew about it. I hefted my bags onto the bed and glanced at the dresser, knowing I should put my clothes away, but wanting the mobility of leaving them in my bags. If shit went south and I had to bail again, I'd be glad I stayed packed. Besides, I wasn't one to get too attached to luxuries like a dresser and my own space. That stuff never lasted long.

The room was quiet and relaxing, and exhaustion weighed heavy on each and every cell in my body. When was the last time I'd had a decent night's sleep? Before the attack sometime. I was tempted to snuggle up with Boots right there and then, but breakouts and cavities were real, so I rummaged through my bags until I located my toiletries. Then I headed for the door with Boots hot on my heels.

This was my first time visiting a biker club. For some reason, I'd expected blaring rock music and wild orgies, but the place seemed calmer than the shelter. No girls were arguing over the bathroom, nobody was talking loudly on the phone in the next room. The hum of conversation and sounds of a game on the television were the only noises drifting up from downstairs. Interesting. I slipped through the door.

A dark-haired biker was leaning against the wall in front of my room. Surprised by his presence, I pulled up short and checked him out. With hair a little on the shaggy side, a toned body, and a strong jaw line, he appeared to be about my age and on the fiery side of smoldering. I'd seen him before. When I'd made the trek to Emily's Jag, he'd been waiting by his bike, watching me like I was a curiosity. He stared at me like that now. His intense, steel gray eyes churned with emotion. I was certain we hadn't been introduced, but he looked at me like my presence physically hurt him. But he didn't look away.

He was the one loitering outside my room. I'd done nothing to him and didn't deserve that look. "Wasp and Emily said I could stay here," I informed him.

He sucked down a breath and dropped his gaze. I got the feeling he could no longer stand to look at me. "I know." His voice was deep and raspy with a slight southern drawl.

"Then..." I glanced back at my door. "Is there something I can help you with?"

"No ma'am."

Seconds ticked by. His gaze jumped around. My shoulder. The wall. His hand. My bare feet. He wasn't leaving, but he wouldn't even look at me. That pissed me off. I marched back into my room, grabbed the key from on top of the dresser, and locked the door before marching past him and down the hall. Once my teeth were brushed and my face was washed, Boots and I wandered back to my room. The hot weirdo was still standing beside my door. This time, as I approached, he pushed off the wall and intercepted me.

"It's not your fault," he said.

Confused, I asked, "What isn't?"

"What that piece of sh..." His jaw ticked and anger narrowed his eyes, still staring at my shoulder. "What Noah Kinlan did to you. It's not your fault." He bit off each word like they tasted foul.

"I know." And I did know. But when nights were too quiet and my brain was too loud, I couldn't help but wonder if there was something I could have done to prevent what happened. I wanted to go back in time and take a different route home. Or cut off my hair and dress like a dude, or knee him in the balls or something. I hated feeling helpless, and Noah had made me feel so damn helpless I disgusted myself.

Finally, the biker looked at me again. "I mean it, Lily. It's not your fault."

"I didn't provoke him. I wasn't wearing revealing clothes. I didn't flirt. I've never even seen the asshole before he jumped me." Something inside me snapped. The fear and anger I'd felt that night came flooding back and I wanted to explode. I hadn't done anything wrong, yet that bastard had still targeted me. "He was bigger. Stronger. His hands..." His hands had been everywhere at once. I couldn't move fast enough to block him. His weight had crushed me against the wooden picnic table bench. I couldn't move him, couldn't wiggle out from beneath him. I shuddered at the memory. "I tried to fight him off, but I couldn't. There was nothing I could do."

The biker's expression softened, and his hands landed on my shoulders, forcing me to meet his gaze. "I know. It's not your fault. I'm sorry. Don't cry. It'll be okay."

I didn't even realize my eyes were leaking until his rough fingertips wiped the moisture from my cheeks. He pulled me to him, wrapping his arms around me. My face landed on his chest. He was warm and solid, and he smelled like rain and sandalwood. I didn't

Taming Bull

even know his name and he looked at me like I hurt him, but he felt safe. I breathed him in as the tears kept streaming down my cheeks. I couldn't even remember the last time I'd allowed myself to cry, and now that the waterworks had started, I couldn't find the valve to shut them off.

"I'm so sorry," the biker muttered. "I should have been there, sweetheart. I'm so sorry I wasn't there for you."

Um, there was no reason this biker I'd just met should have protected me. I didn't know what to say. He was having some kind of moment, and I was confused as hell. While I was still trying to figure out how I should react, he pushed me away from his chest and held me at an arm's length, studying my face.

"You don't fucking give up, you hear me?" he demanded, his eyes blazing.

The anger and passion in his tone knocked me sideways and caused goosebumps to rise across the exposed flesh of my arms. The way he said 'give up' made it sound final. Fatal. Was he worried I'd take my own life? I wasn't suicidal. In fact, I had one hell of a strong survival instinct. It had gotten me away from my family and landed me in a shelter where I'd been steadily pulling myself up by my own goddamn bootstraps.

I didn't give up, I hid.

And now, I was going to fight.

I'd see Noah Kinlan in court, and I'd point him out and tell the world what that bastard had done to me. Then I'd get on with my life.

The biker didn't seem to realize we were on the same page and giving up wasn't an option. He gave my shoulders a little shake. "Promise me you won't quit." His eyes were glassy with unshed tears. I had demons, but this guy… he had the whole devil.

"Okay."

"I'm not playin' with you. Say the words."

Now that he was staring at me, he was so damn intense I could barely stand to hold his gaze. For the first time since my grandma's death, it felt like someone actually cared about me. Like someone was in my corner, cheering me on. His emotions rolled off him in waves that kept threatening to take me under. It was too much, his passion and concern too fierce. I needed to do what he wanted so I could put some distance between us so I could fucking breathe. "I won't give up," I promised.

His gaze took in my features once more as pain filled his eyes. Swearing beneath his breath, he released me. His hands fell to his sides and he straightened. "Thank you."

I immediately missed the heat of his hands and his solid, comforting chest, but I had to get away from him. I opened my door and fled inside, locking up behind me. I crawled into bed and patted the spot by my feet. I didn't know if Boots was allowed on the furniture, but I didn't care. My head was spinning, and I needed the kind of comfort a soft, warm fur baby could give.

I couldn't figure out the biker. My situation seemed personal to him, and I had no idea why. Regardless, I had no intention of giving up.

Boots settled in beside me and I scratched him behind the ears, closed my eyes, and tried not to think about the confusing biker with intense gray eyes. I had no idea he was about to become my best friend and my biggest challenge.

1

Bull

IT WAS THURSDAY afternoon. The Copper Penny Bar and Grill was currently a quiet watering hole for the club with low music and a laidback atmosphere where patrons could grab a decent burger and watch a game or chat with the spattering of bikers seated at the bar. In a few hours, that would all change. The booths, tables, and bar would fill up, and Flint, the manager, would crank up the music, making conversation all but impossible. Bikers and bar goers alike would toss back drinks and do their damnedest to demote shitty workdays into bad memories as security beefed up to keep everyone safe and secure. Sometimes I stuck around for the late crowd, but I always made sure my guest was home safe, first.

Lily was a friend who'd been through more than enough already, and I didn't fuck around with her safety.

Collecting the two bottles of Blue Moon I'd ordered, I thanked Flint and headed for the corner booth where she waited for me. As I moved, the booth's low light bounced off the wall and bathed her in a golden aura, giving her beauty an ethereal glow.

And she was beautiful. So damn beautiful, it hurt to look at her.

Yet, I couldn't seem to look away.

The first time I saw Lily, I thought my eyes were playing tricks on me. She marched down the walkway, heading for Emily's car, looking like my best dream and worst nightmare all wrapped into one spirit-filled five-foot-nothing girl. I hadn't even lasted an hour before I found myself in front of her door under the guise of playing guard duty, but she was safe in the club. My motivation was all about getting another glimpse to assure myself that what I'd seen was real.

It was. Fuck my life, she was very goddamn real.

Years had passed since that first meeting, and being around her was still a sadistic kind of torture that I couldn't refuse, even if I wanted to.

"Hey, brother," Zombie said. He was heading toward the bar, but he stopped and followed my gaze. Waving at the booth and beaming its occupant a big smile, he altered his course and swooped in to give her a hug. "Hey, Lily. How are you?"

Over the two and a half years since Morse and Tap had tracked her down to testify for Havoc, Lily had become the club's little sister. Nobody fucked with her, and any one of us would take a bullet for the girl. Especially after how she'd risked her life going up against Seattle's mayor so Havoc could walk free.

"Livin' the dream," Lily replied with a smile. "How've you been?"

"Good. Just got off work and thought I'd stop by for a drink or six. How's school? You ready to come out and rewire my mom's place yet?"

Inspired by the work Stocks and Monica had been doing around the shelter she called home, Lily had enrolled in classes to become an electrician. She'd been at it for a few months now, and kept surprising us all by the amount of shit she'd learned. Last week, I'd helped her put up a fan in her room. Really, I'd held the base as she cut back frayed wiring and capped the ends of it before mounting a brace and a box. I was worried she'd shock the shit out of herself, but it turned out she knew what she was doing. And her proud smile as she jumped down from the ladder had made me glad I didn't voice my concerns and make her think I didn't believe in her.

"Almost," Lily replied. "We test next week, and then I start my out-of-classroom apprenticeship."

"No shit? Which lucky company picked you up?"

"Puget Sound Electric."

"Atta girl. You'll be rollin' in that fat electrician money soon."

Lily grinned at me. Her smile could light up the entire goddamn bar, which was how she'd earned her nickname. Life had shit all over the girl, but she didn't let it dull her shine. Pretending the sight of her didn't squeeze the air out of my chest and make all the blood flow straight to my cock, I handed her a bottle.

"Yep. Then I'm gonna be Bull's sugar mama." Her eyes sparkled when she looked at me.

"Easy there, firefly." I tipped my beer toward Lily. "I'm a strong, independent man. I don't need no sugar mama. Keep your money."

Zombie barked out a laugh and clapped me on the back. "Well, damn. If it doesn't work with this boring old killjoy, look me up. I'm sure as hell not too proud to let you pay my bills."

Lily always flirted with me, but since nothing could ever happen between us, I did my damnedest to shoot her advances down, even though it almost killed me every fucking time. I knew Zombie was only humoring her, but I still wanted to knock out his teeth. Ignoring him, I faced off with Lily. "Or, you can save your money and buy yourself a dependable car. You're gonna need one to get back and forth to work."

Clearly picking up on my vibe, Zombie took a step back. "It's gettin' too responsible for me around here. You kids have fun. I'm off to shoot the shit with Frog."

Frog waved at us from the bar.

As I settled into my seat, Lily rolled her eyes at me. "Firefly? I told you, I'm not a bug, Bull." Her words resisted the nickname, even as the slight upturn in her lips told a different story. She didn't mind. Not really.

Sliding onto the bench across from her, I took a drink and bought myself some time to check her out. Lily was always gorgeous, but today, she'd put extra effort into her appearance. Her long brown hair seemed shinier. Loose curls drifted over her shoulders ending just shy of her perfect tits. The dark makeup around her hazel eyes made them seem bigger and brighter, and she'd painted her lips in a shade of red that had me envisioning what they'd look like wrapped around my cock. Her off-the-shoulder sweater showed off enough skin to make me hungry for more.

She was temptation and sin, wrapped into a flirty, fun-sized package.

She took a pull from her bottle, and I discretely adjusted myself under the table.

Playing with her bottle, stroking and running her finger down the label, she said, "Thanks for the beer. I'll get next round."

I nodded noncommittally as her active little fingers held my attention. They looked so soft and delicate, but they were deceptively strong. Just like Lily. She'd try to get the next round, but I already had the tab set up, and even if I hadn't, Flint sure as hell wouldn't charge her card. The entire club was proud of her for going to school and trying to better her situation, and we'd do everything in our power to help her succeed. After all she'd been through, she deserved the moon and the stars.

And she was looking at me like I had the ability to pluck them from the sky and hand them to her.

Fuck. Her eyes really did look huge today. How the hell was I supposed to resist her when she kept eyeballing me like that?

"Is something different about your eyes?" I asked.

A smile played on her lips as she leaned forward and blinked slowly. Had her eyelashes always been that long and full? God, she was hot. Being so close to her, with only the table between us, suddenly felt a lot like playing with fire. "No. What makes you think that?"

She was lying, because there was definitely something different. Her big hazel eyes looked softer, more inviting. Whatever makeup witchcraft she'd managed was sexy as fuck. I usually had a hard time looking away from her, but now, the sight of her imprisoned me. I couldn't look away. Hell, I couldn't even remember why I should. Her knees brushed mine, and even through our clothes, the contact sent a jolt of electricity through my veins. Every damn blood cell in my body went straight for my cock.

"Sorry," she said, her smile turning shy as she dropped her gaze.

"Don't..." I coughed to clear my throat. "Don't worry about it."

Her knee brushed mine again and she laughed. This time, it didn't feel like an accident. Her hand landed on my knee. She rubbed, gently. Every stroke felt sexual, and my entire body reacted. Lily had played games like this in the past, but usually I could resist her long enough to make my escape so I could jack off in the safety of my room. Today was different.

I wanted her.

Hell, I couldn't even remember why I hadn't carried her up to my bed and given her what she wanted.

Her hand squeezed my thigh, and I about jumped out of my seat to escape. Angling my legs to press against my bench and save them from her touch, I took a deep breath and tried to get myself under control.

"What's wrong, Bull?" she asked, her eyes full of mischief.

I tilted my head to the side and gave her a hard look. "You know damn well what's wrong. Stop that."

"Stop what?" She rested her head on her hands, the very picture of innocence.

I didn't buy it for a second. Desperate for a distraction, I sucked down another drink and tried to figure out why she'd amped up the game to full blast. Lily hadn't hit on me in months, and I'd been hoping she'd finally accepted the lie that I wasn't attracted to her.

She'd invited me out to drink as friends, and I hadn't thought anything of it. We did shit like this all the time. My guard was down, and I wasn't expecting the little vixen to hit me with everything she had.

If the booth was a boxing ring, I'd be lying on the floor, staring up at the ceiling, and wondering what the hell had just happened. I'd tap out if I thought it was wise, but the smile she flashed me held no mercy. This girl would be the death of me.

The room was too damn hot. Had she somehow fucked with the heater, too? No. It was her sweater. Why was it hanging off her shoulder like that? I could see too much of her soft, silky skin. She needed to straighten her damn clothes and wear them the right way.

Fuck!

My cock had grown so goddamn hard it was painful. I adjusted myself again and rubbed at the back of my neck. My hand came away damp with sweat. "It's warm in here today."

She grabbed at the laminated menu and started fanning herself. "Yeah, it is." Tendrils of her hair flew outward, framing her face. Little beads of perspiration formed on her neck and exposed chest and shoulder, making her skin glisten. I had the craziest desire to lean across the table and lick her clean. Hell, I could almost envision myself doing it. But then my gaze drifted back up to her face, and I reminded myself of all the reasons why that would be wrong.

This was Lily.

She was so far off limits she might as well be in a foreign country. And I lacked a passport and was on a no-fly list. There was no reality in which I'd allow myself to get into her pants.

Lily picked up her beer and put it to her lips. Her pink tongue darted out and licked a drop of pale liquid from the neck, and I about creamed my boxers. She was fucking with me. I knew she was fucking with me, but I couldn't look away. She had my full attention, and she damn well knew it. Her lips wrapped around the bottle and she met my gaze as she drained it. She tugged the bottle from her lips with a pop, and a sexy little moan escaped from the back of her throat.

I was seconds from snatching her out of the booth and dragging her next door to my room. I had to resist.

"Stop that," I said. My voice sounded so low and rough I barely recognized it. I took a sip and tried to calm the fuck down.

"Stop what?" She licked the mouth of the bottle. "This?"

"Yes. Please. For the love of God, stop that."

"Why?" Flattening her tongue against the neck of the bottle, she licked upward to the top, maintaining eye contact with me. "You could always give me something else to lick."

My cock wanted to take her up on that offer so desperately it throbbed, begging. "You know that's never gonna happen." I refused to go there with Lily. No matter how much I wanted her, it could never happen.

She leveled a stare at me. "Why not?"

I shrugged and looked away, trying to come up with a reason she'd accept.

"I want to be with you, Bull, and I know you want me. I can see it in your eyes. I've given you time. I've tried to be patient. Why are you fighting this so hard?"

The determination in her eyes had me second guessing my motives, but I had to stay strong. Nothing good could come from us hooking up. Lily was a lifer, not a temporary fix, and I couldn't promise her forever. Shit was too complicated for that, and I couldn't explain why. But I needed to give her some sort of reason.

"You're like a little sister to me," I blurted out.

"Liar."

"You are. You're like a little sister to all of us. I don't wanna fuck that up."

Her eyes narrowed. "Oh, come on. That is some horse shit. A sister? Is that your final answer?"

Sitting up straighter, I dug my heels in. I needed to sell this lie. I needed her to believe it so she would give up on me. I couldn't give her what she needed, and I didn't want her wasting her life waiting for me. "Yes. I can't see you as anything more. I'm sorry."

She stared at me.

I stared right back, refusing to show even the slightest flicker of how I truly felt.

Anger and pain flooded her eyes and hardened her features. "A sister? That's what you're going with? For real?"

I nodded.

"Great. Fuckin' unreal." She released her bottle and it fell on its side, rolling across the table. Grabbing her raincoat from the seat beside her, she stood. "I can't believe you. You are so full of shit. You might be able to lie to yourself, but I know the truth. Why do you keep pushing me away?"

I dropped my gaze.

"You know what? I'm not interested in your lies, or your friendship, or being your sister. You know what else?" Her eyes brimmed with unshed tears. One leaked down her cheek and she angrily wiped it away. "Forget it. I'm... I'm outta here."

Turning her back on me, she marched toward the door.

I'd finally pushed her away for good, and I felt like shit for it. I should have let her go, but I couldn't. Not like this. Scrambling out of the booth, I hurried to catch her. "Lily, wait. I'll give you a ride."

"No." She halted her steps and poked a finger in my chest. "No way. I'm not going anywhere with you."

I could feel the stares of everyone in the bar on us. Holding up my hands in surrender, I lowered my voice. "I don't want you to walk alone." I didn't care if it was broad daylight, there were still creeps on the street, and I wasn't willing to risk her.

"*You* don't want?" She swiped at another tear. "Oh, by all means, let me move heaven and hell for what the mighty Bull wants. That's what we always do, right? Whatever *you* want. Do you even give a single fuck about what *I* want?"

"Lily, I—"

She held up a hand, silencing me. "No. I'm done listening to you." She surveyed the patrons at the bar. "Can anyone else give me a ride home?"

Nobody spoke.

"Lily, I—"

Her shoulders dropped. "Please?"

Carly, one of the bartenders, appeared to be coming onto shift. She glanced at Flint and he nodded. "I'll take you, Lily."

More tears rolled down her cheeks. Each one felt like a knife to my chest. "Thank you."

"No problem. Come on." Glaring at me, Carly draped an arm over Lily's shoulder and steered her toward the door.

I watched them go, knowing I'd screwed up big time, but I didn't have a clue as to what I should have done differently. I couldn't be with Lily, and it was high time she accepted my limitations on our friendship.

2

Lily

IT WAS RAINING out, and my boots were muddy, so I bypassed the front door and went around to the side entrance of the shelter. Using my individual code on the recently installed electronic lock, I let myself in.

"Hello?" Monica called from the next room. A friend who'd appointed herself as my adoptive mom when she and her biker husband, Stocks, had taken over management of the shelter, Monica was the most amazing woman I'd ever met. She'd lost an arm while home on leave from the Air Force, ending her career, but she didn't let that slow her down one bit. She'd just altered her dreams, found the man of her life, and made life her bitch despite her disability. I wanted to be just like her someday.

"Hey." I kicked off my rubber boots and removed my raincoat. A row of crowded hooks lined the right side of the mudroom wall, and I found the least full one and hung my coat up to dry. "It's just me."

"Uhoh. You're home early. Not a good sign."

No, it wasn't. Still fuming from my talk with Bull, I marched into

Taming Bull

the adjoining kitchen and found Monica preparing dinner. Feeding eight grown adults meant she spent a lot of time chopping veggies and kneading bread. The rest of us helped when we could, but the purpose of the shelter was to provide a landing pad while we sought schooling and jobs to better our lives. Most of us only made it home long enough to eat and sleep.

Today, Monica was preparing a roast roughly the size of a small country to feed our horde. Crowded with potatoes, carrots, celery, onions, garlic, she had at least a quarter of a cow rubbed in spices and ready to go. The sight of it made my mouth water. She opened the oven and paused, arching an eyebrow at me. "Debrief me, babygirl."

Operation Make Bull Admit His Feelings for Me had been a total flop. I rolled my eyes so hard they dried out. Bad idea. My vision was still a little blurry from the optometrist, and for a second, I didn't think my eyeballs would roll back into place. Luckily, they did, giving me the chance to shift my focus back onto the important topic of my non-existent relationship with Bull. "Ohmigod. He is such an asshole."

"That good, huh?"

I snorted. "I don't get it. He likes me. I know he does. He just refuses to admit it. Why? Is there an award he's trying to win for keeping his hands off me or something? Has it become an Olympic sport? Do I have the plague?" I raised my arm and looked it over. "Smallpox? Is my flesh falling off?"

She fought a smile and picked up the roast. It had to be heavy, but I didn't dare offer to help. Monica had been mastering her prosthetic, and she sure as hell didn't need me doing shit for her. "I see no leprosy or smallpox. Just a beautiful, frustrated young queen." She slid the giant pan into the oven, and then gestured toward the dining room. "Come. Sit. Tell me all about it."

With Monica and Stocks at the helm, the once dilapidated old shelter had come a long way in the past two years. We'd been renovating the hell out of the place, replacing the roof and flooring, updating sketchy old lighting and electrical boxes, and painting everything in warm, comfortable colors. Monica had named it The Castle, because she only took in queens who'd had their crowns knocked off by life. She gave us a safe place to sleep, provided three square meals, and pushed us off our asses, encouraging each of us to do something amazing with our one wild and precious life.

And it was impossible to make excuses to a one-armed badass who courageously practiced what she preached. Trust me, I'd tried.

Although Monica was all about straightening our crowns, I didn't think The Castle was a fitting name for the shelter. I'd never been in a castle, but they seemed cold and pretentious to me, and our home was anything but. Warm, cozy, and full of yummy food smells, the shelter was now every good thing I remember about my grandma's house. After she passed away, I never thought I'd experience this sense of safety and belonging again, but Stocks, Monica, and the rest of the Ladies First crew had made it happen.

I owed them more than I could ever repay, and I couldn't wait to finish my apprenticeship so I could start giving back.

Sitting in the chair beside Monica's, I dropped my head, planting my face against the cool surface of the table, and sighed dramatically. "The friend zone is a black hole from which there is no escape."

Monica chuckled. "So says Google."

A recent internet search for ways to get out of said friend zone had yielded that answer. At the time, I'd refused to accept the wisdom of Google as fact, but it was proving to be far truer than I cared to admit. This black hole was like a commercial grade vacuum and I was nothing more than a speck of dust. "It's worse than I could have imagined. He didn't friend zone me, he... he little sister zoned me."

Skepticism filled Monica's eyes as she watched me. Then she shook her head and let out a low chuckle.

Her laughter stung. "It's not funny," I said. "The man I'm desperately and irrevocably in love with sees me as his little sister.

If anything, this is tragic. My life is over. I might as well go find a convent and become a nun now."

"Our little Lily is always so dramatic." Visibly struggling to control herself, she patted my hand affectionately. "I've seen the way he watches you. If he's sister zoning you, it's some sort of backwoods Ozark kind of family."

I snorted, cautiously hoping she was right. Replaying the scene from the bar in my mind, I'd had him. There was nothing *brotherly* about the way Bull had responded to my flirting. He wanted me.

So, why the hell wouldn't he take me?

"Fucking sister zone. As if the friend zone wasn't bad enough," I lamented.

"Sister my ass." Monica started singing the dueling banjos from the movie *Deliverance* in a compilation of do-dos. She was a ridiculous human being, and just being around her made me feel better. "Goddamn, you play a mean banjo," I quoted.

"I bet you can squeal like a pig," she quoted back.

"What's going on here?" Stocks asked, his tall frame filling the doorway to the living room. Tall, with dark hair and the kind of muscles guys develop through service in the Marines, dozens of hours of physical therapy, and two years of hardcore home remodeling, Monica's husband was handsome. He was also one of the best men I'd ever known. Crossing the room to join us, he brushed a kiss across Monica's forehead. She closed her eyes, looking so damn blissful from his affection it made my chest hurt. The way his fingers slid down her arm, maintaining every second of contact they could until he stepped away said far more than any sappy poem or declaration of love.

Monica looked from him to me and raised her eyebrows. "He got a real pretty mouth, ain't he?"

I cracked up. No matter how bleak my love life was, I wasn't dead yet, so that was funny.

"Quoting *Deliverance*, huh?" Stocks asked. "Must be serious. One of you better start squealing like a pig."

Monica winked at him. "Later."

"Gross," I grumbled.

As Stocks puttered around the kitchen, Monica watched me like she was trying to figure something out. Finally, she asked, "Are you high?"

"What? No. Why would you even ask that?" Drugs had never been my thing, and Monica knew why. Drugs would also get my ass kicked out of the shelter, and I didn't relish the idea of being homeless.

"Your pupils are huge."

"The lighting in here sucks," Stocks said, coming to my defense. "I was thinking we should add some LED recessed lighting across the ceiling here." He pointed up.

"It's not that dark." Monica's stare didn't relent. "What's going on with your eyes?"

I dropped my head into my hands, preparing to admit yet another failure. "I'm not high. I had an eye doctor appointment before I met with Bull. I read that guys are more attracted to girls with big pupils, so I let the doctor dilate them."

"I don't think that's a thing." Stocks took a glass down from the cupboard and filled it with milk.

What did he know? Monica had hooked up with him the first time she'd met him. She'd spotted him across the room and decided he was gonna get lucky. I'd heard their story more times than I could count, and I was certain he didn't need to learn any secrets of the opposite sex to win her over. "It *is* a thing. Trust me, I've been researching."

Monica laughed, shaking her head. "I can't believe you got your eyes dilated for a guy. Never heard that one before."

"First of all, I didn't do it *for* him. It's been years since I had an eye exam, and it just so happened that my appointment was right before I was scheduled to meet up with Bull." Okay, I'd scheduled the appointment around our date so I could see if Bull would find me more attractive with my eyeballs dilated, but she didn't need to know that little detail.

Her amused expression told me I wasn't pulling any wool over her peepers. "So, you had your eyes dilated. What else?"

"The better question is, did it work? Did Bull find your dilated eyes irresistible?" Stocks popped one of Monica's home baked cookies into his mouth and chewed.

"My girl doesn't need to have her eyes dilated to be irresistible. Bull just needs to pull his head out of his ass." Monica narrowed her eyes at Stocks. "And dinner's in the oven. Better not ruin your appetite, Butter."

They came up with the weirdest nicknames for each other. This particular endearment was due to Stock's level of smoothness, or lack thereof. Smooth like butter, he was not, yet she found his attempts endearing.

"This is just an appetizer." He snagged another cookie before joining us at the table. "You know how I am, babe. Whatever spread you put before me, I'll eat." He winked at her.

I pretended to gag at the innuendo.

Monica flashed him a wicked smile and patted my hand. "What else, Lily."

"I made eye contact, held his gaze, brushed his knee with mine. I even patted his leg."

"And?" Monica gestured for me to continue.

"Isn't that enough?"

"I know you're holding back. You can't play a player, babygirl. Spill."

Some things were too embarrassing to share with the woman who was more of a mom to me than my biological mother had ever been. But I didn't see a way out of it. Monica was relentless, and wouldn't give up until I'd told her all my dirty little secrets. I knew she only wanted to help, but I suddenly wished I'd never told her anything about my attraction to Bull. My cheeks heated and I dropped my gaze. "I tried to seduce him with my beer bottle."

She gasped. "Dear God. Please tell me you did not deep throat a bottle in the Copper Penny."

"That's about enough of that," Stocks said, heading for the door.

"Nope." Monica pulled out the chair on the other side of her. "You sit your fine ass down. You're gonna help us figure out your boy."

Looking like he'd rather be anywhere but the kitchen, Stocks reluctantly slunk over and collapsed on the chair, watching us both like we were about to start talking about menstrual periods or something.

"I didn't deep throat a bottle," I told them both, regaining a smidgeon of my dignity. "I only licked it a tad."

Stocks shook his head at me. "Kid."

I hadn't been a kid in a long ass time, but he was the closest thing to a father figure I had, and I didn't want to disappoint him. Or myself, for that matter. "I know, I know." My head went back to my hands, trying to hide my shame. "Not my finest moment, but I don't know what else to do. I've dropped hints, practically molested him when he was teaching me self-defense…"

"I gotta hand it to you, that self-defense ruse was crafty," Stocks admitted.

"Thank you." I nodded. "He was sporting some serious wood, so I know he was feelin' me but…"

Stocks held up his hand. "Please. No talking about another man's wood. I'm tryin' to be cool, but there's only so much I can handle."

Monica snickered. "You're doin' great, baby."

"I better get one hell of a reward later."

"Anyway…" I busted into their little side conversation before they could gross me out again. "I'm out of ideas. Hell, Google's out of ideas. I know he's into me, but for some reason the stubborn asshole refuses to admit it."

Something flickered across Stocks's features, disappearing almost as quickly as it arrived. I caught it, though, and so did

Taming Bull

Monica. I'd seen the expression before, when he'd dropped a wrench—a literal wrench—on one of Monica's soufflés and didn't want to fess up due to threat of life and limb.

Why would Stocks look guilty? Unless...

"What do you know?"

He threw his hands in the air. "What do you mean?"

I pinned him in place with a glare and made my question as specific as possible. "Do you know why Bull won't give me the time of day?"

His eyebrows rose and his gaze swept the room like he was looking for the best escape route.

"Oh my god, you do know something." Monica hit the table. "I can't believe you've been holding out on us. You know how important this is to Lily."

Stocks grabbed Monica's hand. "Baby..."

"Don't you 'Baby' me. You might as well start singing, because whatever you know... we're gonna get it out of you sooner or later."

"It's not that simple. You two are asking me to roll over on one of my brothers."

The guarded hope I felt was reflected back to me in Monica's eyes. Without saying a word, we made a pact. Stocks really did know something, and we had to play it cool and weasel the information out of him before it was lost to us forever. It was game time.

"I didn't say 'roll over,' did you say 'roll over,' Mon?" I asked.

She shook her head, fighting back a smile and gave him the most innocent look I'd ever seen her fake. "No mention of rolling over here. Of course, I could roll over later if you'd like." She leaned closer to him, sliding her hands over his shoulders and to the back of his neck. "I could roll over a lot, but that all depends on you. Do you want me to... roll over for you, baby?"

Stocks swallowed. His Adam's apple bobbed with the effort, and I knew we had him right where we wanted him. He'd do anything for Monica. "I feel teamed up on. We should go down to the humane society and pick up a male dog, so I have one ally in this house."

He did know something, and it was so good he was trying to change the subject. Leaning forward, I laced my hands and plopped my chin down on top of them, giving him my full attention. "What do you know?"

Glancing at Monica one last time, he replied, "It might be nuthin'."

Monica gestured for him to continue.

"Just drunk talk among the club brothers."

We both stared at him, waiting.

Finally, he let out a sigh. "There was a girl."

His words hit me like a sucker punch. "Was?" I asked.

He nodded. "They were high school sweethearts, and when Bull joined the Navy she went away to college."

When he didn't offer more information, I was tempted to jump across the table and strangle it out of him. Instead, I took a breath and used all of my tapped-out self-control to stay cool. "And?" I asked.

"She committed suicide while he was serving."

Monica gasped. "What? Why?"

Stocks shrugged. "They said she was raped, turned in her rapist, and nobody believed her. I don't know what happened. Maybe he was harassing her or something."

I had so many questions. I'd been raped by the son of one of the most powerful men in Seattle. I'd been afraid for my life, but I'd never considered taking it. There had to be more to the story than that. Bull was in the service when it happened, but didn't she have a family or friends to reach out to? Where had her people been? If she'd reported it, why hadn't the cops helped her? "Did she try to contact Bull?"

Stocks shook his head, frowning. "No. They said that's what messed him up. They'd been together for years and had plans to get married when he got out of the service, but she never even told him she was attacked."

If I ever convinced Bull to be my man, I'd tell him everything. Even the stuff he didn't want to know. This girl had him and had left him in the dark. I couldn't make sense of her actions. "Why didn't she tell him?" I wondered aloud.

Stocks threw up his hands. "Your guess is better than mine."

"Please tell me her rapist is getting ass raped in jail," Monica said.

"I asked if there was a trial, but the guys didn't know."

Desperate for more information, and grabbing onto this flimsy thread of information with both hands, I pulled up a web browser on my phone. "Do you know her name?"

"Nope."

Dammit. "When did it happen?"

"I'm guessing shortly before your situation, Lily." Stocks's eyes softened as he gave me a supportive smile. "Some asshole in his squad mouthed off about it to Bull, and he put the dipshit in the hospital. That's how Bull earned himself a dishonorable discharge and ended up here."

How had I never learned of this? Bikers gossiped worse than most of the girls in my high school, but nobody had said shit to me about Bull's past. Of course, I hadn't thought to ask them, knowing how close they all were. "Do you know which college she attended?" I asked.

"Nope. All I know is what I told you. And Zombie and Buddha were pretty plastered, so I'm not sure how much of it is true."

Thinking, I tapped my cell phone to life. "If they were high school sweethearts, she must have been from Shiner, too."

"Shiner?" Monica asked.

"Bull's hometown. It's in Texas, kinda between San Antonio and Houston." I was having a hard time with the idea of Bull having a high school sweetheart. He was mine, dammit. No other woman was supposed to have his heart. Especially not a dead one. Did he still love her? Is that why he warded off all my advances? How the hell was I supposed to compete with a ghost?

"And you know about Bull's hometown, because...?" Monica asked.

Typing in the year of her death, town name and 'college girl suicide,' I started my search. "He goes home for Christmas every year. I wanted to see where he'll be taking me after he finally succumbs to my advances and admits we're destined to be..." The rest of the sentence died on my lips as a picture of Amber Kent appeared on my screen. Suddenly, all my dreams of a life with Bull came crashing down around me.

"Lil?" Monica asked, her tone concerned. "The blood just drained from your face. You're even whiter than normal. What'd you find?"

My lips moved, but no sound would come out. All I could do was stare at the image and silently curse the universe. What horrible thing had I done to deserve this? Reincarnation had to be real, because I must have been a mass murderer in another life. Bull's reluctance to give me a shot finally made sense. No wonder nothing I'd tried had worked. How painful was the sight of my face for him? How could he even stand to be around me? Everything clicked into place. Now armed with all the information, I fully understood that I'd been fighting a losing battle.

It didn't matter what I did, the man I was hopelessly in love with was forever out of my reach.

"What?" Stocks asked. Reaching over, he slid the phone out of my hand and spun the screen around so he and Monica could see it. "Oh. Holy shit."

Yes. The holiest of shits.

Eyes wide, Monica looked from the phone to me and back to the phone. "Ohmigod. Bull's dead girlfriend is your doppelgänger."

Yep. My life sucked. I dropped my forehead to the hard wooden table and silently admitted defeat.

3

Bull

EVERY FRIDAY NIGHT, the Dead Presidents held a weekly meeting referred to as church. Unless your ass had a rock-solid reason for missing it, attendance was mandatory and the business we discussed was considered sacred. Unlike other motorcycle clubs, we didn't participate in illegal shit like running drugs or guns, but we still valued privacy and followed basic club protocol. Nothing said within the walls of our chapel left the room, an assurance that made it easier for brothers to share ideas and air grievances with abandon.

This room was where the club had first voted to do whatever it took to find struggling veterans.

A lot of impromptu therapy had taken place within these walls.

A couple fights had broken out.

Once, I'd even fallen asleep in a pew, waiting for brothers to work their shit out so the meeting could be released. Nobody left until everyone could shake hands and walk out side-by-side, like brothers. It felt a lot like a giant, barely functional family.

I'd grown up in a small family. Dad managed a warehouse, and

Mom volunteered at the church. They were solid people who worked hard and prayed harder. I was a good kid who did what I was supposed to do, and they mostly left me to it. I loved and respected the hell out of my parents, but we never really connected.

My relationship with my sister wasn't any better. Four years my senior, she never wanted to leave the safety of our small, familiar hometown and couldn't understand my dreams of joining the Navy and sailing around the world. Now happily married, with a baby on the way, we couldn't be further apart if I lived on the fucking moon.

Shit was never supposed to be so strained between us, but Amber's suicide, and my reaction to it, changed everything.

My carefully planned four years of service, travel, and self-discovery before I settled down with my high school sweetheart to start my own family came to a screeching halt. I couldn't see past the insults hurled at my dead fiancé by a man who was supposed to be my brother-in-arms. Unable to cope with losing her, I tried to kill him and landed myself in the brig. My refusal to apologize and get my shit together got me tossed out of the service on my ass. No matter. I had no regrets, and if I ever saw that motherfucker again, I'd break more than a few ribs and an arm.

My family expected me to come home, but Shiner, Texas held too many memories of the life I'd lost. I couldn't face Amber's parents any more than I could face my own. Hell, even my conversations with Mom and Dad were nothing but surface bullshit as we talked about the weather and news, dancing around the giant fucking elephant in the room between us like it was our goddamn job.

I couldn't go home.

Branded as a loose cannon with a dishonorable discharge, opportunities weren't exactly beating down my door.

My Grandpa had met Link's dad, Jake, the former president of the club, during his stint in the Army. When I had nowhere to go, Gramps reached out to Jake and secured a place for me in a veteran only motorcycle club in fucking Seattle, Washington. I thought

Taming Bull

Gramps was off his rocker when the plane ticket showed up in my email, but it turned out he knew exactly what he was doing. The biker lifestyle was just the culture shock I needed, and their acts of community service helped me to see that even a dishonored sailor with a dead future could still do some good in the world.

Here, I had people, and a goddamn purpose I could get behind.

And, I had Lily. Or, at least I'd had Lily before she'd told me off and stormed out of the Copper Penny. Tugging my phone from my pocket, I opened my messaging app and reread our last conversation.

Lily: Is it just me, or is the word asleep really weird? No other word in the English language adds an a to the beginning of a verb to turn it into an adjective. I mean, you're not 'anap' or 'aeat.'

Me: I was 'anap' before you sent me this bizarre text. Where do you come up with this shit?

Lily: What can I say, I'm a thinker. We still on for tonight?

She was always sending me shit like that, and I kept every last message. We usually texted multiple times a day, but my phone had been quiet since Thursday. I wished I could go back in time and cancel our get-together. Then things between us could go back to the way they were before.

Lily was my closest friend, and I missed her random, crazy ass so damn much.

"Any other old business?" Link asked from the front of the room where he was seated with the rest of the board.

When nobody spoke, our president nodded. "The floor's open for new business."

I'd been sitting by the back door, waiting for this very moment. As if I needed an additional cue, Wasp, the club's vice president, grinned, and waved at me. Being the observant bastard he was,

Link picked right up on our unspoken communication. I could feel the president's gaze burning up my back as I headed out into the hall to retrieve the loaded dolly Wasp had hidden in the janitor's closet. I returned just in time to catch the tail end of whatever other new business the club had coming up.

"Morse will be updating our website with the information later this week for individual donations," Link said, standing at the end of the executive table like he always did when he had something important to share. "Eagle's starting a list of volunteers who can make the rounds to local businesses to pick up donations. If you've got time to help, get your name on that fuckin' list. I know I don't have to tell you all this, but when we make deliveries, I want all hands on deck. It's good for the community to see your ugly mugs and know not every motherfucker on a sled is a goddamn degenerate."

He was talking about our annual toy drive. It was one of several community driven events we took part in every year. The biker stereotype was real, and we fought tooth and nail to break it. When I first became a prospect, I asked Link why he led a motorcycle club if he didn't want to be typecast as a one-percenter. He looked at me like I was a special breed of moron and explained that riding was in his DNA. Running guns and drugs wasn't. The two weren't mutually exclusive.

I didn't understand what he meant until I made my first club ride up to Canada to visit an ally club. There was nothing in the world like the wind in your face and the open road under your tires, surrounded by brothers who had your back no matter what. I'd never felt so goddamn alive and accepted in my life.

Being a biker wasn't about breaking laws, it was about freedom and family.

After the months I'd spent locked up in the Naval Consolidated Brig, I never thought I'd feel those gifts again. I sure as hell wasn't worthy of them.

"What else we got for new business?" Link asked, giving me and

Wasp the side-eye. Wasp was always trying to get a rise out of the prez, and the sheet-covered package in my possession looked hella suspicious.

"Oh, I got something for you, brother," Wasp replied, making his words sound all levels of threatening. He stood and gestured me forward, grinning like the ringmaster of his own personal circus. Not sure what that made me. Probably a fucking trained monkey for helping him with this crazy idea. "Come on, Bull, what are you waiting for? Bring it up here."

Everyone turned and watched as I rolled my covered offering up the aisle between the packed benches. Whispers and the occasional chuckle drifted around the room as people speculated about what Wasp was up to now. The left wheel squeaked loudly, and I winced.

"Jesus, Wasp," Eagle, the club's secretary swore. "You'd think our head bike mechanic could figure out how to grease a fuckin' wheel."

"Just adds to the anticipation," Wasp replied with a wink.

By the time I reached the board table, Link had his arms folded, and was scowling at Wasp. "This better not be another fuckin' waste of club time."

Wasp considered it his personal duty to keep the prez grounded and humble, and he didn't give a shit whose time he wasted in doing it. Hoping I wasn't about to get my ass kicked for my role in the VP's latest antics, I rolled the dolly to a stop beside him and got the hell out of there, putting as much distance between myself and the prez as possible. As I sat, Wasp grabbed the sheet and tugged, dramatically revealing his surprise.

It was a wooden podium. Wasp had found it on some used furniture site. It had been beaten to hell and ready for the recycle bin, but the wood was sturdy. Wasp had tasked me with the project, and I'd tightened a few screws, sanded, stained, and sealed the distressed pine, and banded it with a steel frame to cover the dents and cracks of old age. Now it was a beautiful piece of furniture, complete with an angled top, electrical chase, and two interior shelves.

I'd never considered furniture restoration to be in my wheelhouse, but I felt nothing but pride as I looked over my work.

Link's eyes were full of appreciation and apprehension as he eyed the piece. "A preacher's podium?" He arched an eyebrow at Wasp. "It's beautiful, but what the fuck is it for?"

Wasp grinned. "Figured since you like preaching at us so much, you should have your own pulpit, Prez."

Ah, the punchline. Wasp couldn't help himself. Laughter erupted around the room as our vice president egged the room on.

Link glared at Wasp for a solid minute. Then the corner of his lips slid up into a smirk. Shaking his head, he replied, "Such a fuckin' wiseass."

"What?" Wasp asked, positioning the podium a few feet away from the table, facing the room. "Fuckin' helpful is what I am. I saw a need and I took care of it. Downright thoughtful. Resourceful even." Wasp smacked the wood and the hollow sound echoed. "Bull, I can't believe how good this looks. Bet it didn't even look this good brand new. You got a gift, brother."

His praise felt like too much. I ducked my head and thanked him.

"Get up here, ol' man." Wasp gestured Link over. "You wouldn't want all of Bull's hard work to go to waste, now, would ya?"

Link reluctantly joined Wasp behind the podium. He ran his hands over the wood and nodded to me. "You did a fine job, Bull."

More praise I didn't know what to do with. "Thank you."

Wasp grinned. "You look good up there, Preach, er... I mean, Prez."

"Amen," Havoc, the club's sergeant at arms, added straight-faced.

More snickers floated around the room.

Having grown up in church, I've seen my share of preachers. With long hair and covered in tats, Link didn't remotely fit the image. "Bunch of fuckin' clowns," he muttered, but he stayed behind the podium. "Now, can we quit the bullshit and get back to business?"

Wasp took his seat and gestured for Link to continue.

"Anybody got any *real* new business?" Link asked. When there was no answer, he pulled his phone out of his pocket and typed something into it before returning his attention to the group. "Nobody? All right. I've got something. We have a visitor who wants to check the club out before he throws his hat in to become a prospect. He was stationed out of Fort Lewis."

"Army or Air Force?" Buddha asked. Officially known as Joint Base Lewis-McChord, the base located just south of Tacoma housed both military branches. Since it was originally an Army only base, most of the locals and old timers still referred to it as Fort Lewis.

"Army," Link replied.

The door opened, and a dark-skinned man peered in. His gaze scanned the room before landing on Link. "Permission to enter?"

Oh yeah, this guy was fresh out of the service.

"Come on in." Link waved him forward. "We're pretty relaxed around here. Just a bunch of assholes cracking jokes and shit as I'm tryin' to lead church." To the group, he added, "Dead Presidents, meet our prospective prospect, Tavonte Jones."

"Tay is fine," Tavonte replied as he paused by the board table.

"Why don't you come up here and tell us a little about yourself?" Link asked.

Tavonte marched up to the podium and Link stepped aside, giving him room. "What do you want to know?" the newcomer asked.

"Where you're from, family details, what your job was, any skills or shit. Whatever you want people to know about you."

Tavonte took a moment, and answered, "I was born and raised in Nashville. My mom and my little sister are still there."

"And your dad?" Link asked. His eyes had softened, making it clear he knew the answer and it was a rough one.

Tavonte didn't reply.

"Go ahead," Link urged. "We're all family here. We keep no secrets."

"Except Tap," Morse blurted out.

Everyone but Tap laughed. The former intelligence officer flipped Morse off.

When the room grew quiet, Link nodded to Tavonte.

"Army," Tavonte answered. "He died in Somalia when I was a baby. I don't remember him."

Someone swore.

"Damn shame," Havoc said.

Tavonte looked uncomfortable. Link watched him, as if waiting for more details, but Tavonte kept his mouth closed.

Jake stood, his eyes full of emotion. "We understand and appreciate your family's sacrifice. We're glad to have you here, brother."

Jake's brother had joined the service alongside him, but he never came home. Still officially listed as MIA, Link's uncle's disappearance had been the driving force behind the formation of the Dead Presidents MC. They say the hardest part of serving is coming home. Jake wanted to create a safe place for people like his brother to come home to, so they wouldn't have to fight this battle alone.

Link must have finally recognized Tavonte's discomfort and took pity on him. He stood and clapped the man on the back. "Tay here served as a 91B." For those of us who weren't Army, he added, "A wheeled vehicle mechanic. Bull, tomorrow can you show him around the shop before your shift starts?"

I usually went into work early and sat around trying not to think about Lily until it was time to take the tow truck out. Showing the new guy around would be a welcome distraction. "Yessir."

"Good. Let's adjourn for the night and go show this young buck a good time." Link picked up the gavel and hit the table, releasing us.

Everyone stood and drifted toward the front of the room where they congregated around Tavonte, asking him questions and welcoming him to the club. The guy looked a little shell shocked, and I didn't want to add to the chaos around him, so I slipped out of the meeting.

Located in a renovated old fire station, the clubhouse was a massive building. The main floor held the chapel, offices, bathrooms, an industrial kitchen, and a common area full of sofas, televisions, pool tables, dart boards, and a fully stocked bar. The chaos in the chapel would eventually drift down the hall to the common area, where drinks would be poured, stories would be shared, and shit would get loud. Glad to be ahead of all that, I made a beeline for the bar.

A few ol' ladies were sitting around chatting on the sofas, waiting for their men to emerge. I didn't have to even look to know Lily was in the group. I could feel this fucked up connection we shared pulling me toward her. I ignored it for as long as I could before giving in and glancing in her direction. Hard glares stared back at me. Lily had no doubt filled them in on what happened between us last night, and now I was in deep shit with the broad squad.

Great. Just what I fucking needed.

Sure, they were only looking out for Lily, but dammit, so was I. In fact, the more I thought about it, the more I realized allowing Lily to flirt with me over the past two years had been like leading her on. It wasn't fair to either of us. The best thing I could do now was to lock that shit down and make it clear we had no future. It would be hard as hell, but I'd manage. I had to, or I'd go fucking crazy and do something unforgivable like fuck her senseless. Then shit would get really complicated. Doing my best to ignore them, I slid onto a barstool.

Shari, one of the club whores, was manning the bar. She

greeted me with a smile, for which, I was grateful. Either news of my misdeeds hadn't reached her, or she was staying neutral. "Hey, Bull, what can I get you?" she asked.

"Just a beer, please."

She reached into the fridge and retrieved a local Belgian. Popping the cap, she handed the bottle over and leaned close. Lowering her voice so only I could hear, she said, "Better watch yourself. I think the ladies are plannin' your funeral."

Feeling the heat of their glares, I made a conscious decision not to look over my shoulder and nodded. "Surprised you didn't spit in my beer or something."

Her smile widened. "I'm neutral in all matters of war and the heart. Just call me Switzerland."

Tilting my bottle toward her in salute, I said, "Thank you, Switzerland," before taking a drink.

"You betcha."

The common area started filling up. I turned on my stool and watched as Havoc strolled in. He went straight to the sofas and kissed Julia on the forehead before taking his son from her. Link and Eagle weren't far behind. When I'd first prospected, the club didn't have a single child in it. Now, we needed a fucking daycare.

My gaze involuntarily drifted to Lily. Fuck. My resolve hadn't even lasted a full ten minutes, but I couldn't help it. I clearly had a type, and she matched it. Seated on the sofa beside Monica, I could only see from her shoulders up, but it was enough to knock the wind out of me. She was so damn gorgeous I couldn't force myself to look away. Watching the couples with their babies, her eyes filled with longing, reminding me of why I couldn't be with her.

She wanted the forever I'd already promised to someone else.

Even now, I couldn't help but compare the two of them. Lily's eyes were a little rounder, and Amber's cheek bones had been a little softer. Where Amber was sweet and innocent, Lily was fierce and jaded. Amber's career choice was driven by the desire to help people—she wanted to work with special ed kids. Lily chose the electrician route because it offered the best pay for the least amount of schooling.

Regardless of their differences, I couldn't stop thinking about how awkward it would be to take Lily home. My parents would see my dead girlfriend and think I'd lost my damn mind. Amber's folks would probably have a coronary. Hell, the whole town would be whispering about how I couldn't have Amber, so I brought home her twin.

And they wouldn't be wrong. Lily's likeness to Amber was what had drawn me to her.

It wasn't fair to Lily, and I needed to give her space so she could get over me and find a man who could give her everything. A man who could take her home and be proud to introduce her to his family. A man who still had a future left to offer.

Determined to make myself scarce until she took the hint and stopped hitting on me, I picked up my beer and headed for the stairs.

I didn't feel much like partying anyway.

4

Lily

STUNNED, I STARED at the cashier, willing different words to come out of her mouth. She had to be mistaken. She couldn't possibly be serious. "What do you mean you don't serve breakfast anymore?"

The look she gave me questioned my intelligence, sobriety, and grasp of basic English. Slowing her words as if decelerating her speech pattern would increase my chances at understanding, she repeated herself. "We no longer serve breakfast."

No. This couldn't be happening.

"It isn't profitable. Corporate made the call to pull it from our menus." She pointed at the menu on the wall behind her. "We don't even open until ten now."

Which explained why she'd been unlocking the doors when I arrived. I really should have put two and two together sooner, but I was far too heartbroken to tell time or read a menu. I needed a sausage, egg, and cheese breakfast bagel to improve my quality of life. The promise of that cheap but delicious comfort food was the only thing keeping me going right now, and I didn't give a single fuck about the restaurant's profitability.

My happiness depended on that goddamn bagel, and if I didn't get it, I ran the risk of devolving into a sniveling ball of pathetic single cat lady piss. Nobody wanted to see that. It wouldn't be a good look for me.

I wanted to go full on Karen and make a scene, but it wasn't the restaurant's fault my life had gone straight down the shitter. Not at fault, but they should have held the power to fix it via chewy, greasy comfort food. I was desperate. The last bit of internet advice I'd followed was a piece titled, 'Absence makes the heart grow fonder.' It was proving to be complete and total bullshit. Despite the recommendation of relationship gurus everywhere, giving Bull space had clearly not made him miss me and throw himself at my feet.

Nor had it made me want to club him over the head and force my love upon him any less.

It had been two weeks since I'd last talked to the asshole, and I was no closer to getting over him than I had been when he'd sat across from me, sweating bullets and pretending not to watch me lick the neck of my beer bottle like a lollipop. I'd thrown a fit and told him I didn't even want to be his friend before storming out of the Copper Penny.

That's me, the picture of maturity and grace.

I couldn't help it. Bull just brought out my crazy and encouraged it to tango with him. We'd done this song and dance so many times I felt like I was following a script, but that was the first time I'd taken my flirting so far. I'd pushed hard, and he'd repelled even harder. So now, I was giving him space so he could miss my awesome self and come begging for my forgiveness.

So far, this plan sucked ass. I'd seen him a few times, but it was like he was trying to outmaneuver me. To out-ignore me.

I didn't even know which of us was avoiding the other anymore.

Then this morning, I'd woken up early and decided this bullshit had gone on too long. It was past time to swallow my pride and get my friend back. Raiding my piggybank until I collected enough cash for the expensive bakery that made the best doughnuts in Seattle, I'd taken a dozen of their most popular delicious, sugary fat bombs to the club's auto shop. Bull's shift started at nine, but I arrived at a quarter 'till, knowing his obsessively early ass would already be there.

Thinking back about it made my fists clench in anger.

Tiffany, a beautiful blonde with enhanced, giant boobs she liked to display in tight, scooped-neck tank tops, despite the autumn weather, was working the counter. Sauntering up to her like I belonged there and wasn't at all intimidated by her superior boob size, I held my head high, clutched the box of doughnuts to my chest and asked for Bull.

"Sure, Lily, take a seat. I'll get him." She picked up the phone and spoke into it.

I had too much nervous energy to sit, so I paced beside the counter and waited. Seconds stretched into minutes as I second guessed myself at least a dozen times—once for every doughnut in the box—and almost left. Twice. But above all else, Bull was my friend. I missed him. I needed to apologize and make things right between us.

Bull was talking to the new guy when he walked through the side door and into the room. I didn't want to be disappointed by his expression when he saw me, so I turned away and counted. One, two, three, four... His steps faltered. Turning at the sound, I caught the longing on his face as he hungrily devoured my appearance.

Pride flared in my chest as I inwardly high-fived myself for his reaction. It had taken me an hour to perfect this sunset eyeshadow I'd seen on YouTube. My long, brown hair was styled in soft waves, and I was dressed in a sexy mid-thigh sweater dress and knee-high black boots. The outfit had almost cleaned out my bank account, but the look on his face was worth every penny.

Like a sister, my ass.

He wanted me as much as I wanted him. Desire burned in his eyes and flared his nostrils. He looked more like a determined Spanish Fighting

Bull than a Bullmastiff, and I was here waving the red cape and begging him to charge.

"Lily." He said my name much like a curse. Like he'd just stubbed his toe and that was the first thing that came out of his mouth. Then, the invisible wall he kept between us went back up, shielding his emotions. He met my gaze, and icy indifference stared back at me.

Son-of-a-bitch.

"What are you doing here?" he asked.

The eye-fucking he'd greeted me with had filled me with hope, but this frosty reception shattered it. Struggling to recover, I tried not to notice the pity in Tiffany's eyes as she pretended not to watch us from the counter. I needed to fix this... needed him to hear me out and give me a chance. Give us a chance.

"Can we... talk for a minute?" I stammered, every ounce of uncertainty I felt leaking into my words.

"It's not a good time right now. I gotta get to work."

I glanced at the clock on the wall. He still had twelve minutes. I only asked for one, but I wasn't about to beg for it. Fine. He was pissed at me. No big deal. I still had one more trick up my sleeves. Opening the box of goodies, I spun it around to face him, banking on the way to a man's heart being through his stomach. Bull had a sweet tooth. I knew this, and I intended to exploit the hell out of his weakness. Since he wouldn't give me the courtesy of a private conversation, I'd just have to say my piece in front of everyone. Fine. I'd sacrifice my pride.

"I... I wanted to apologize for the other night. I brought you doughnuts."

His jaw ticked. Without even looking at my tasty offerings, he replied, "You were right, and you didn't do anything wrong."

I was right? About what, exactly? And why did he seem so angry about it?

Before I could ask, he said, "Thanks for the doughnuts. I'll make sure everyone knows they're out here."

I didn't say they were for everyone; I specifically said they were for him. Yet, he made no move to take one. I watched Bull, willing the ice wall he'd erected between us to melt. Our friendship was bigger than one stupid fight. Silently begging him to say something more, I waited. But apparently, he was done speaking.

Were we finished? Had he thrown in the towel on me for good?

The new guy watched Bull like he'd just sprouted a second head. I understood his confusion. Bull's behavior was so out of character, I didn't have the faintest idea how to respond. It was like my crush had given up on warding off my advances, and now he was actively trying to push me away.

Oh hell no.

I stepped forward to either lay Bull out or give him a piece of my mind—I wasn't sure which—and the new guy met me and offered his hand. "Hey. I'm Tay."

I wanted to weave around him, but Grandma's old etiquette lessons kicked right in. Besides, he was rockin' a nice, genuine smile that deflated a little of my outrage. I met his firm but friendly handshake with my own, and gave him my brightest not-about-to-punch-Bull-in-the-stomach smile. "Lily. It's good to meet you."

"Likewise. Thanks for the doughnuts. It was really thoughtful of you to do that for us." He elbowed Bull in the side. "Right, Bull?"

Bull shook out of his icy stupor. "Yeah. Thanks. You shouldn't have."

He added a little too much meaning behind that last part for my comfort. My chest hurt and my eyes stung, but I ignored the pain and held myself together. "The Dead Presidents have done a lot for me and..." My gaze drifted to Bull who seemed tense as hell and was doing his best to ignore us. I forgot what I was going to say. I wanted to shake him until that stupid wall came crumbling down. "It's no big deal."

"I gotta get to work," Bull said. Without even looking at the doughnuts I'd spent more than I could afford on, he turned and stormed off.

I wanted to cry. No, I wanted to hit something, and then cry. No, I wanted to kick Bull in the shin and make him cry. Licking my beer bottle may have been taking our flirting game too far, but come on. He couldn't still be pissed at me for that. Our friendship had lasted years, and he was going to throw it away over something so stupid?

Tay watched Bull retreat, and then offered me an apologetic smile. "I... Sorry? I don't... He... Uh..."

I felt his confusion in my soul, really, I did. "I get it. Don't worry about it." *Forcing a smile, I added,* "Have a great day." *Then I got the hell out of there before the tears building up behind my eyes could stream down my face.*

Okay, so I wasn't staying completely away from him and probably should have given absence a little longer to let his heart grow fonder. I'd tried, but I was only human.

And internet relationship gurus could officially kiss my ass.

As far as I could tell, this entire mess was all their fault. If I hadn't listened to their stupid advice on how to catch my man, Bull would still be my friend. Of course, I'd still be stuck in that black hole of a friend zone, but at least we'd have something.

Now, all I had was this gaping hole in my heart.

After leaving the shop, I'd wandered around the city until my feet brought me to the front door of this restaurant, promising broken heart relief in the form of food therapy. The tapping of the cashier's fingertips brought me back to the present. No breakfast sandwiches. No carbs to stanch my bleeding heart. Right. Only it wasn't right. It was so not right I couldn't even wrap my mind around it. There had to be give and take, highs and lows, ups and downs. That's how the universe worked. If I couldn't have the man I wanted, I should at least be able to consume my bodyweight in the greasy, chewy goodness of my preferred comfort food. I needed one damn positive for all this negative.

The cashier must have seen the soul-crushing despair in my eyes, because she hurried to apologize. "Sorry. There's nothing I can do. We don't even have the supplies to make it anymore. We threw out what didn't sell before we made the change."

They threw it out? Like it was nothing? Like it didn't have the power to fill this gaping hole in my heart. What kind of monsters would do such a thing?

Was Bull throwing *me* away?

"Can I get you anything else?"

There was a line forming behind me, and she needed to move me along to help the others. Why were they even here? Nobody should be eating lunch this early. No, I didn't want some burger and fries. I wanted a goddamn breakfast sandwich like an American. But since I couldn't have that, I dropped my head and ambled out of the restaurant. Needing someone to lament to about my craplousy day, I called Monica.

"Hey babygirl, what's up?" she answered.

"Burger Villa no longer serves breakfast."

"Um... Okay?" The confusion in her voice made it clear I'd have to give her the full story.

"It's important, Mon. We're talking life or death serious, here."

"Gotcha."

Her casual tone said she didn't fully grasp the severity, but I plowed ahead anyway. "It's this restaurant I frequent, and they have the most delicious sausage, egg, and cheese bagel—crispy on the outside and chewy inside, with the perfect combo of greasy cheese and seasoned sausage to make my broken heart feel better. But. They. Stopped. Serving. It. I desperately need this sandwich so I can eat my feelings. If I don't get it, I'll have to do something crazy, like deal with Bull's rejection like some grown ass adult, and I'm not ready for that kind of responsibility in my life. Not at all. I passed my tests and now I'm getting a real apprenticeship which will lead to a serious job. I have maxed out my threshold for adulting."

"All adulted out, huh?" she asked.

"Exactly. I need that chewy, greasy, delicious distraction to keep me young and depression free."

"I see."

Was that laughter in her voice? "No, I don't think you do. I think you're mocking my pain." An unexpected tear leaked from my eye and rolled down my cheek. I swiped it away and scoffed at the moisture on my fingertips. Okay, I *was* possibly overreacting. Crying over a breakfast sandwich felt like taking things too far.

Especially when I didn't want that bagel nearly as much as I wanted Bull. Knowing why he kept rejecting me only made me want him more.

Amber had broken his heart.

Her suicide had crushed him so completely, he hadn't even slept with any of the club girls. Lacy said he'd taken her up to his room once. They started making out, but when she went for his zipper, he shut down and asked her to leave. Drunk as all get out, he'd still been faithful to his dead girlfriend. Now, I couldn't stop imagining Bull, all alone and lonely in his room, waiting for me to come and rescue him from the ghost of relationships past. It was tragically endearing the way he clung to his ex, but that bullshit needed to stop. He needed me, and no thickness of icy walls or bone chilling cold shoulders was going to stop me from saving him from himself.

"If you swing by the store and pick up bagels and sausage on your way home, I'll make you one of those breakfast sandwiches," Monica offered.

"What about eggs and cheese?" My question came out like a pout, but I didn't care.

"We have those."

I considered throwing a toddler-sized fit and telling her it wouldn't be the same, but Monica didn't deserve my tantrum. And I really did want a bagel. "Okay," I replied. "Thank you."

"I gotchu, boo," she replied before hanging up.

Feeling marginally better, I hurried to the closest grocery store and picked up the necessary ingredients, adding ice cream and a bottle of wine to my basket just in case the breakfast sandwiches didn't do the trick. While leaving the store, I almost tripped over a leash that connected a brown-haired little boy to a mid-sized dog.

"Oh! Are you okay?" A woman asked, hustling to my side.

"Yeah." Righting myself, I adjusted my bag of groceries. Nothing had fallen, and I'd somehow managed to avoid face-planting on the sidewalk. Good thing, because with the way this day was going, I'd probably just curl up in a ball and die right there. "I'm good."

"Johnny, I told you to be careful. You can't let BB stray like that. If you can't hold him, I'll have to take his leash."

Johnny had to be about six or seven. His big, round eyes were red like he'd been crying, and if my grandma had seen how far his lower lip was sticking out, she'd tell him to pop it back into place before a bird came along and shit on it. Gross, I know, but the woman who'd raised me had given up the pretense of being a lady long before I arrived on the scene. Scowling at the woman I assumed was his mom, Johnny tugged on the dog's leash and pulled BB closer, revealing a handwritten sign that read, "Free to a good home."

Suddenly, Johnny's swollen eyes and bad attitude made sense. I squatted down to pet the dog they were looking to rehome. He was a beautiful grayish-cream color with dark markings around his snout and eyes. His square jaw and boxy, muscular build screamed pit bull, but he had the sad eyes of a hound. "You're getting rid of this handsome guy?" I asked, nodding to the note.

"No!" Johnny snapped.

"Yes," the woman replied, giving him a stern look. "We have no choice. I'm Shelly, by the way." She offered me her hand, and I stood and shook it.

"Lily. Why do you have to get rid of him?" I asked. He didn't look like a biter and was far too calm to be aggressive.

She stepped away from Johnny and the dog, and I followed. Lowering her voice, she replied, "My ex-husband's divorce attorney is better than mine. We have to sell the house and our new apartment doesn't allow dogs." Her eyes hardened and steel coated her words as she looked at her son's heartbroken expression and added, "I could kill John for making me do this to our boy. He gets off scot-free and I get to be the bad guy once again."

The dog was watching me, his sad, round eyes pleading for

Taming Bull

help. I wondered if he knew they were offloading him. "You said the dog's name is BB?" I asked.

"Yes. He's a beabull... a beagle pit bull mix. BB just kind of stuck." Hope brightened her tone. "Are you interested? You can change his name if you don't like it."

The generosity of Ladies First was the only thing keeping me from being homeless. I'd passed all my knowledge classes and was scheduled to start my paid electrical apprenticeship on Monday, but my starting wage wasn't even enough to rent a cardboard box in Seattle. Especially not if I had to put down a dog deposit. Monica and Stocks had made it clear I was welcome at the shelter until I got on my feet. We'd even tossed around the idea of me staying longer and renting my room to help them out, but I didn't think it was the type of arrangement that would allow me to bring home a pet. Still, Stocks had mentioned wanting a boy dog...

"Are you having a hard time getting rid of him?" I asked.

"Yes." She sighed. "He's a four-and-a-half-year-old pit mix. Everyone wants a puppy—and not a pit—but, puppies destroy everything and need training. BB's a good boy. He's well-trained, excellent with kids, and very mellow. He needs a good home where he'll be loved and appreciated." Her eyes were heavy with tears, and she blinked and looked away. "I'm sorry. This is harder than I thought it would be."

I couldn't even begin to imagine what she and Johnny were going through. The dog was tugging at every single one of my heartstrings, and I wanted nothing more than to help him and this struggling family out. Promising to return, I excused myself and stepped away to make a phone call.

Monica answered on the second ring. "Hey, I thought you'd be home by now. I'm all prepped and ready to make the best damn breakfast sandwiches you've ever tasted."

God, I loved her. "You're the best, and I will be home shortly, but remember how Stocks was talking about wanting a male dog?"

"You mean when we were ganging up on him and forcing him

to roll over on Bull?"

As much as we'd denied it at the time, that was exactly what we'd done. "Yeah. That time. Well, there's a dog outside of Safeway that really needs a home. He's beautiful and mellow, with these big hound eyes that have melted me into a puddle of goo. There's this little boy, and his parents are getting a divorce..." Emotion thickened my words, making me turn my back on the sight of Johnny sniffling and hugging BB.

"Wait. I'm confused. Thirty minutes ago, you were all torn up about some breakfast sandwich. Now, you want a dog?"

"You don't sound confused. I mean, you pretty much nailed it."

"But how did we get here?"

"Is that really important?" I asked.

"Call it curiosity."

"Technically, it's your fault."

She chuckled. "Oh, I can't wait to hear this."

"It was your suggestion. You told me to stop by the store. I practically tripped over the dog coming out. It's like the universe threw him directly into my path to soothe my broken heart. He's animal therapy. Seriously, Moni, if you saw him, you'd understand."

"I don't know, Lil. This seems like the kind of big decision we should discuss as a group. What if someone's allergic to or afraid of dogs?"

"All of the girls fawned over Boots when we went to the fire station. Nobody was allergic to him. I'll keep Brahma in my room if you want. He's four, well-trained, and good with kids. I'll take him with me when I move out."

"Brahma?" she asked. "As in Brahma like the bull? Is this about Bull?"

"No." Okay, maybe a little, but she didn't need to know that. "They call the dog BB because he's a beabull, but his coloring reminds me of a Brahma bull, so I figured he can keep the initials so it's not so confusing for him. Plus, he'll have a much tougher sounding name."

"Oh, God. Stop. Your logic is beginning to make sense to me, and I've never been more terrified in my life."

"Don't fight it. Embrace the crazy. It's easier that way. You should see this guy. He's so sweet and lovable and I have a plan to help the little boy feel better."

And, Brahma would keep me busy. He'd take my mind off Bull and give me something to direct all my time and energy into.

"Please, Moni."

"How badly do you want this dog? Quantify this decision for me."

I'd grown up with dogs, so I knew all about their massive amounts of poop to clean up, and I was willing to take on the commitment. I glanced in the bag of groceries, trying to think of the best way to make her understand my obsession. "I'm letting ice cream melt as we speak."

"Shit. That *is* serious."

"Yeah. I have four days off before I start my apprenticeship. Four days that I can either mope around the house and drive you crazy, or get to know my dog."

"This sounds like blackmail."

She was considering it. I had to force myself not to jump for joy. "You call it blackmail, I call it honesty."

"I really hate it when you mope."

I fought a smile, knowing I had her. I couldn't believe it. "Yeah, me too. You have the power to keep all that moping at bay. Moni, you could be a hero."

"Goin' a little overboard now, don't you think?"

"Hey, go big, or go petless." Now I just sounded like a dork.

Monica huffed out a breath. "Promise you'll clean up after him?"

Ohmigod, she was going to let me get him. "Yes! Of course." I couldn't have kept the excitement from my voice, even if I'd wanted to.

"I mean it, Lily. If I find one pile of shit in my yard, he's gone, and I will draw and quarter you."

Wow. Her threats escalated quicker than normal. "Isn't that the penalty for treason?"

"Don't question me."

"Right. Drawn and quartered. Totally reasonable. I promise."

"I can't believe I'm letting you talk me into this."

"Deep down, you're still going for that purple heart." Monica had been a fighter pilot who'd been wounded, but not while in action. It was a touchy subject that I poked at every chance I got, hoping someday it wouldn't be sore anymore.

"Yeah, yeah. Just get home so I can meet the mutt."

Hanging up, I pocketed my phone, adjusted my bag of groceries, and hurried back over to Johnny. Kneeling beside him, I sat my bag on the ground and smiled. "Hey."

He didn't respond.

"I have an idea that might allow you to still hang out with BB, if you're interested."

That got his attention. He looked up at me with eyes full of hope and swimming with tears. "What is it?"

I probably should have run my suggestion by his mom first, but screw it. I'd gone too far to back down now. "If you let me have BB, I can give your mom my phone number and we can meet up sometimes so you can still see him. As long as it's okay with your mom."

Shelly watched me from a few feet away. "You'd be willing to do that?"

"Yes. Absolutely. I don't want Johnny to have to lose him completely. There's a park not far from here. I'd be totally down to meet up there once a week."

Johnny's eyes grew round as he looked from me to his mom. "Can we?"

She swallowed back emotion and nodded. Then looking to me, she said, "Thank you, Lily."

5

Bull

"WHAT THE FUCK man?" Tavonte asked, his expression full of disgust, like I had some sort of airborne disease and had just sneezed in his face.

Keeping my gaze on him—and trying my damnedest not to watch the sway of Lily's fine ass as she walked away—I feigned ignorance. "What?" I asked.

Over the past two weeks, Tavonte and I had spent enough time together to form a mutual respect. There was a bro-code that clearly stated he needed to let me handle my own business and stay the fuck out of my personal shit. But the way his eyes narrowed told me he hadn't gotten the memo. "Lily." He belted out her name like it was a complete sentence, accompanied by the universal hand gesture for *what the fuck?* Just in case I still didn't get his message. I did. Loud and clear. I wanted to punch myself in the face for the way I'd made Lily's smile falter and hurt flood her eyes.

I felt like the biggest asshole on the planet.

But I was only trying to protect her. To protect both of us.

I shrugged, still pretending I didn't know why Tavonte was spitting and gesturing like a fucking cartoon character. The situation sucked, but my hands were tied. Lily and I couldn't be together, and it was high time we both accepted it and moved on.

But I missed her.

Over the past two weeks I'd picked up my phone at least a dozen times to text or call her, only to remember that I couldn't. I had to let her go. Life wasn't the same without her. She was like an amputated arm I kept trying to engage, only to be reminded that it was gone. I wondered if she felt the same. Then she'd shown up with doughnuts to bridge the ever-widening chasm between us, but I couldn't let her do that.

Hurting her now would save us both a world of pain in the future.

As Tavonte followed me back through the waiting room's side door to the auto shop, I could practically feel the heat of his anger simmering just beneath his skin. This thing between me and Lily had nothing to do with him, but he was fully engaged. "You got nuthin' to say for yourself?" he asked.

No. I'd never been much of a talker, and I didn't see how spilling my guts would improve the situation. "What's there to say?"

He gaped at me. "That the way you always treat ladies?"

I'd been expecting some sort of confrontation, but it still stung. He should know me better than that by now. He should trust me. "There's a lot of shit you don't know," I replied, hoping like hell he'd drop it.

"Oh yeah?"

His eyes challenged me to fill him in and redeem myself. He didn't want to believe I was an asshole. In his place, I'd probably do the same thing. No. If someone treated Lily the way I had, I would have just clocked the piece of shit. No words would have been necessary. I wanted to say or do something to wipe the look of disgust off his face, but it wouldn't help. The story was convoluted and crazy, and I probably couldn't make him understand if I tried.

Instead, I met his glare. "Yeah. Mind if we stop gossiping like a couple of teenaged girls and get to work?"

I watched that mutual respect we'd been building shatter in Tavonte's eyes as I climbed into the tow truck and buckled up. Yeah? Well, he lost some of mine, too. Guys shouldn't ride each other's asses about matters that had nothing to do with them.

The fuckin' bro-code, man. Learn it. You should have my back.

Out of the corner of my eye, I watched him wage a silent war with himself. He marched toward the truck, froze, and then turned toward the door and took a step. It was like he was torn between ripping off my driver's side door to demand answers and storming out of the shop.

Why was he so invested? He didn't even know Lily. Maybe some asshole had once taken advantage of his mom or little sister and he was projecting? Whatever. He needed to get over it and either get in the truck or leave. Just as I rolled down the window to tell him as much, he yanked open the passenger's door and barreled into the seat. I expected another outburst, but he didn't say shit, just stared straight ahead. I doubted we were done with the conversation, but I was damn grateful for the respite, no matter how brief it proved to be.

I probably shouldn't be too surprised he was riding my ass. Tavonte was a good guy who wasn't shy about pointing out shit he didn't agree with. Last week, he'd asked Wasp and Rabbit why we didn't extend our towing operations to twenty-four-seven.

"It's a financial risk," Rabbit replied with a shrug.

"It's an opportunity to expand," Tavonte countered. "The shop's busy, and the tow trucks are rarely parked. Want me to look into it? Run some numbers for you?"

I didn't know what 'running numbers' entailed, but it sounded about as fun as a root canal. Tavonte seemed eager for the task. It was like he wanted to prove himself, but that didn't make a lick of sense. If he wanted to earn the respect of the club, all he had to do was put on the prospect patch. But for some reason, he hadn't yet.

Wasp gave him a lopsided smirk. "Yeah. Show us what you got."

Wasp liked Tavonte. He wanted him in the shop with the other mechanics, but Link made it clear that Tavonte was on the truck with me until he committed to prospecting. When Tavonte presented his market research, showing the club could employ two more dispatchers, two more drivers and provided reasonable projections for profitability, Wasp had tried to force the prospect cut over his shoulders.

Still, Tavonte resisted.

Smart, outspoken, and determined, the chances of him letting me off the hook about the way I'd treated Lily were about as good as a hen house surviving a fox invasion. I kept bracing myself for an attack, but it didn't come. In fact, he didn't say shit to me until I merged onto the freeway, headed out to pick up our first tow of the day.

"You know what I hated most about joining the Army?" he finally asked.

Suspecting his question was connected to my situation, I didn't want to answer. But his question got me thinking about all the things I'd hated about the service, and curiosity finally got the best of me. "No. What?"

"The waste. Growing up, Mom worked her ass off to keep the lights on and make sure me and my little sister stayed fed, but shit was always tight. We didn't waste anything. Some of the kids at school used to get the bread crusts cut off their sandwiches. I asked Mom to cut off my crusts once." He chuckled and shook his head, caught in the memory. "Thought she was gonna rip my head off. You can be damned sure I never asked her again. When she put something on my plate, I ate every bite. Practically licked the plate clean. She made sure we never went without, but there were times I could have eaten more. Times I went to bed still feeling hungry. Then I joined the service and was blown away by the sheer amount of shit the government wasted. I mean, I understood why they couldn't fuck around with the chances of food poisoning, but watching all the untouched food go straight into the trash... man, that was rough. My first night on KP, I had to throw away an entire chocolate cake. All I could think about was struggling families... kids going to bed hungry... parents hustling to put food on the table... and here I was dumping a perfectly good cake in the trash. It made me sick to my goddamn stomach."

The service was known for waste. Thrown out food, trashed weapons and vehicles because it was easier and more convenient to buy new, the waste was unreal. Sure, we created jobs and helped the economy, and only taxpayers lost in the grand scheme of things, but it was still ridiculous. My parents were well off, and I'd never gone to bed hungry, but the government's waste had been a real thorn in my side, too. I nodded.

"I don't know what kind of shit you and Lily are dealing with, but the way you looked at her before she saw you..." Tavonte let out a low whistle. "Fuck, man. It felt like we were all intruding. I expected you to run over and scoop her up in your arms and spin around like a sailor who just got off a boat or some shit like that."

His romantic cliché description threw me off guard. I barked out a laugh and shook my head. "You watch too much TV."

"Probably." His tone sobered. "But it gets a little lonely out there. Especially when you're between action and nobody but your mom seems to care if you come home alive."

Silence settled between us as I wondered what all Tavonte had seen and done while in the Army. He'd served for ten years, plenty of time to build memories and rack up nightmares. My time had been cut short. I hadn't seen any real action, and I'd always had someone special waiting for me to come home.

Well, until I didn't.

"Lily apologized," Tavonte said, dragging me back to the present. "I don't know what mortal sin she committed to piss you off. Maybe she cheated on you or blew all your money or something?"

He was fishing. I kept my mouth closed and my eyes on the road, hoping he'd just shut the fuck up and let it drop.

"I always knew I was heading for the service, so I didn't date much in high school. I fucked around, but I made it clear I wasn't looking for anything serious. I had a few dates while in the service, but they weren't what I expected. I wanted to talk and make a connection. They wanted a transaction. Flowers and dinner for a fuck. Buy a gift, get laid. It's like everyone's so busy trying to get the best end of the deal they don't even try to connect anymore. It's bullshit, man."

I chuckled. "You sound like a goddamn romantic."

He shook his head. "I sound like a lonely mother-fucker who's sick and tired of having to pretend I'm just lookin' for pussy because that's what society expects from me. And because assholes like you give me shit for it."

That wiped the grin off my face. "I'm not an asshole."

"I didn't think you were. But then Lily got all dolled up, brought you donuts, and asked to talk. She's trying to connect. That girl showed up and she's willing to fight for you. Do you have any idea how rare that is? Everyone's so fuckin' jaded and scared of getting hurt, they don't put themselves out there like she did. And you turned her away. I can't tell you how many men—including myself —would kill for a woman willing to fight for them. She's like that perfectly good chocolate cake. You look at her like you want to eat the whole damn thing, and you don't even know what's inside. I bet it's your favorite filling. Whatever you like: raspberry, cream, mint, whatever. But instead of digging in, your dumb ass is throwing her away. Don't fuckin' waste that, man. You may think another will come along, but I'm tellin' you, it's rare as shit."

I wanted to argue but couldn't. Lily had nothing to apologize for. Her only mortal sin was in her striking resemblance of my dead ex-girlfriend, an offense we could never overcome. Lily didn't deserve to live in the shadow cast by Amber's ghost, but life wasn't fair.

Lily also didn't have money to blow on shit like doughnuts for the crew. But she was a giver. That's just who she was, and no number of well-meaning objections from me could change that fact.

Damn, I missed her.

I'd always meant to keep her at an arm's length, but over the past two years, she'd weaseled past my defenses and became my best friend. I missed hanging out with her, playing darts, explaining football, shooting pool, and talking for hours about nothing at all. Lily usually talked; I listened.

I missed the sound of her laughter.

Tavonte didn't get it; I wasn't wasting what we had, I was trying to protect us both from what we could never have.

Lost in my thoughts, I almost missed my freeway exit.

By the time I realized it, the off-ramp was ending. I braked, swerved, and barely made the exit. Tavonte watched me with a shit-eating grin, no doubt enjoying the way he'd gotten into my head. Ignoring him, I focused on finding my tow.

In the Big Lots parking lot, sat a baby blue 1994 Buick LeSabre. The disabled vehicle was parked a good three feet away from the parking block, like it petered out just shy of the finish line. I pulled up behind it, slid the tow truck into park, and got out. Tavonte fell into step behind me. An elderly woman with tight, gray curls sat in the driver's seat with a white-knuckled grip on the steering wheel. Worried that two strange guys approaching might do her in, I gestured for Tavonte to hang back. He'd already read the situation, though, and was moving away.

Her driver's side window was down about a quarter of an inch, so instead of knocking and potentially startling her, I stepped loudly and cleared my throat. Keeping her hands on the wheel and her gaze locked ahead, she showed no signs of hearing me.

"Ms. Moore?" I asked.

She jumped.

I'd done everything I could think of to avoid startling her, but I still felt like an asshole. Giving her the same disarming smile I grew up using on the elderly folks at my parents' church, I pointed to the nametag on my uniform. "Hi. I'm Bull, I'm with Formation Auto Repair. Heard you had a little car trouble and I'm here to give you a tow."

She studied me, surprise filling her grey eyes. "*You're* with the tow company?"

Unsure of why she was having trouble accepting my employment, I nodded enthusiastically. "Yes, ma'am." I pointed to truck parked behind her. "Got my truck ready and everything. If you want to step out of your vehicle, I'll get this ol' beauty hooked up, take her back to the shop, and see if we can't get her workin' again."

She lowered her glasses to the tip of her nose and looked me over. I was young for a tow truck driver, but I was certified, and despite my distracted, late exit from the freeway, I was a damn good driver. I was preparing to defend my age when her gaze drifted down my body.

The mischievous gleam in her eyes made it clear she sure as hell wasn't verifying my employment. "By this ol' beauty, you talkin' about me or my car, young man?"

She was flirting. Shocked, I stared at her. I needed to reply, but didn't know how to answer. Sure, I'd had customers flirt with me before, but none that were my grandma's age. Flirting back seemed inappropriate, but leaving her hanging was just plain rude.

While I struggled to come up with a response, she struck again. "What's a woman gotta do to get the full service around here?" Just in case I'd missed the inuendo, she waggled her thin gray eyebrows at me suggestively.

I'd been trying to make her feel safe and comfortable, and she'd fucking knocked me on my ass. Unable to help myself, I belted out a laugh. "We're not that kind of a service station, ma'am, but let's see what we can do about your car."

"Damn," she said with a huff. "It was worth a try."

As I helped her out of her vehicle, Ms. Moore copped a feel of my bicep, obviously preferring that to the forearm I'd presented her with, even though she had to reach over her head to hold on. I pretended not to notice her diabolical grin or the way her fingers probed the contours of my muscles. Even as we reached the safety of the curb, she kept a death grip on me, like I was a new toy she was afraid someone would take away.

"Is there someone you can call to pick you up?" I asked, wondering how I was going to remove her from my arm.

"I suppose I could call my daughter, but she's working. Can't I just ride with you to the shop and have her pick me up on her lunch break?"

"Sure." I gestured Tavonte over. "Ms. Moore, this is Tay. He's helping me out today."

She gave Tavonte the same half-starved appraisal she'd given me. A small pink tongue whipped out to wet her lips. "Oh my. There's two of you. Vanilla and chocolate. It's like one of those swirl ice cream cones with the best of both worlds."

The fairy tale *Little Red Riding Hood* came to mind, and I couldn't help but think Charles Perrault had gotten his story wrong, because this little old lady *was* the wolf. She wasn't big or bad, but she was definitely hungry. Her eyes took on a glazed-over look, and I didn't even want to know what kind of fantasies she was conjuring up.

"Hello Ms. Moore. Pleasure to meet you," Tavonte said. His gaze cut to me and silently screamed *what the fuck?*

I shrugged. Her smile widened as she released my arm and clung onto his. He was closer to thirty and fresh out of the service, and the gleam in her eyes said she wasn't opposed to giving dark meat a try.

"The pleasure is all mine," she replied.

Chuckling under my breath, I made my escape and hitched her Buick up to be towed.

6

Lily

IT HAD BEEN a long time since I'd owned a dog, and I'd forgotten how much shit the furry little beasts required. Shelly opened the back of her minivan to reveal a fluffy, round dog bed; a flattened, medium-sized kennel; a Costco-sized bag of dog food; a variety of chew toys; a box of peanut butter flavored treats; food and water dishes; a pooper scooper; a manilla envelope full of important papers; and a roll of plastic poop bags. The lot of it must have cost her a fortune, and although I didn't have the funds to replace it, I recommended she sell it to recoup some of her investment. I mean, her life and marriage were crashing down around her, so I figured she could use the money.

"Nope." She gave me a watery-eyed smile. "It goes with BB. It'll make his transition easier, and it's our way of saying thank you for being willing to work with us on visits."

So, there I stood, mentally calculating the number of blocks between the grocery store and the shelter and wondering how the hell I was going to get all this shit home.

"If you want to swing your car around, we can help you load it up," Shelly offered.

But as my grandma would say, I didn't even have a pot to piss in, much less a car. "I walked today." And every day, but she didn't need to know I was a transportation-impaired loser. Owning a dependable ride was stage three of my ten-stage plan to become a real fucking adult, and I was currently teetering between stages one and two. Wheels would come, eventually, but I needed to get down the whole kick-ass electrician apprentice gig, first. I couldn't even consider a monthly car payment until steady paychecks were rolling in.

Shelly offered to take me home, but no matter how kind and friendly she seemed, she was still a stranger. The shelter served as a safe haven for homeless young women between the ages of eighteen and twenty-five, a lot of whom were hiding from something or someone. When Stocks and Monica had taken over, they'd called in the club's tech guys, Morse and Tap, to scrub Sacred Heart Women's Shelter from digital existence. Stocks had removed the sign, and for all intents and purposes, the old shelter was no more. To the outside world, the recently renovated building was now a huge house occupied by a big, mixed family.

Looks could be deceiving.

Ladies First, the non-profit run by the ladies of the Dead Presidents, had purchased the shelter, and was steadily improving the way it operated. We no longer accepted walk-ins. Even if homeless women managed to miraculously find us, they sure as hell weren't allowed entry until Ladies First screened them. It was harsh, but a necessary evil since the philanthropic ol' ladies insisted on helping women get out of bad situations. Abusive exes didn't always respect things like restraining orders, and risking the safety of the shelter's tenants was not an option.

After all the precautions everyone had taken to protect our safe haven, leading a stranger to the doorstep would be a dick move.

And I was no dick.

Instead, I did what I always did when I needed help; I used a lifeline and phoned a friend.

"Hey, Lil, what's up?" Stocks asked by way of greeting. The road noises in the background clued me in on the fact he was driving. Since he'd never even hear the phone ring on his bike, he had to be in his truck, which was perfect for my purposes.

"Are you out running errands?" I asked.

"Yep. Just picked up the new moldings for the upstairs hallway. Why? You need something while I'm out and about?"

"Yeah. A lift. I'm at the Safeway by the house and I... uh..." I didn't know if Monica had told him about Brahma yet, and I didn't want to drop the bomb over the phone. I also didn't want to lie. "I over-shopped." There. That was honest. Mostly. "Can you pick me up?"

"Sure. I'm only a few blocks away. Hold tight. I'll be there in five."

Thanking him, I hung up and waited with Shelly. When Stocks arrived, he did a double take at my "over-shopping," but didn't say a word as he loaded Brahma's stuff into the back of his truck beside the molding. Stocks drove an early 90's Chevy 1500, that had been covered with more rust than paint when he'd purchased it. With the help of the club's auto shop, he'd managed to breathe life into it, but no amount of money could resurrect it completely. It was basically a zombie truck, moving, but not necessarily alive. He only used it when he needed to haul stuff for the shelter.

The door creaked as I opened it and settled my bag of groceries on the bench seat. I turned and watched—trying not to bawl like a baby—as both Shelly and Johnny said tearful goodbyes to the dog. We'd already set up our first visit for the following weekend, which, I suspected, was the only reason Shelly was able to pry Johnny's fingers from Brahma's leash.

"You'll see him again soon," she promised, handing the leash off to me.

Johnny was barely holding on to his emotions, so I hurriedly

Taming Bull

coaxed the dog into the truck before the boy could lose his shit. I climbed in the truck, and Brahma settled his butt by my feet, putting his head on my knees and staring up at me like I had just become the center of his universe. His pure, unbridled adoration did wonders for my recently stomped on heart.

Bull might not love me, but the new guy in my life sure as hell did.

Stocks settled in behind the wheel and studied the dog. "I have so many questions."

He looked more curious than upset, so I gave him my widest smile. "Surprise! It's a boy. Congratulations, you now have an ally."

"Oh, so this is for me?"

I nodded wildly. "Absolutely. Stocks, meet Brahma. Or BB for short. And he's a lot of dog for one person, so we should probably share him."

Chuckling, Stocks bent to pat Brahma on the head. The dog let out a contented sigh, and turned to lick Stocks's hand in thanks. "Aww. What a good boy."

"Don't let the sweet face and gratuitous kisses fool you. He's a ferocious pit bull mix that will help you guard the castle and keep the residents safe."

Stocks gave Brahma a skeptical eyebrow raise. "Ferocious, huh? You don't say?"

Brahma blinked at me, also seemingly unconvinced. If there was a ferocious cell in his body, it had either slipped into a coma or been sacrificed to the doggy god of cuteness.

"Does Monica know you're bringing home a dysfunctional guard dog?"

I covered Brahma's ears against the insult. "Don't worry, BB, dysfunctional is a requirement. You'll fit right in." To Stocks, I added, "Do you think I'm suicidal? Of course she knows. If I don't clean up after him, she intends to kill me. Creatively."

"That sounds about right. Well, I'm not mad about him. Growing up, I always wanted a dog, but my parents weren't animal people. They still aren't." Stocks gave Brahma one last scratch behind the ears before starting up the truck.

I had the support of the man of the house. Now we just had to win over Monica. On the way home, I gave Brahma a quick pep-talk, filling him in about the lay of the land. He didn't exactly promise not to poop in the house, but he did nudge my hand every time I stopped petting him. "You'll get all the loves in the world as long as you kiss up to Monica when we get home," I told him. I shouldn't have worried. As soon as I led him inside, he wandered straight to the queen of our castle, sat at her feet, and gave her the same worshipful devotion he'd given me.

He was a smart little traitor.

"How am I supposed to be mad about that?" she asked, her expression softening as she gestured at the dog. He rolled over and showed her his belly in a surefire show of his pit bull viciousness. "Oh, God, he's just a big teddy bear, isn't he?" She bent and scratched his underside until his leg kicked so hard against the floor he sounded like a rabbit. "That's the spot? Aww. You're such a good boy, aren't you?"

Introductions made, I turned my attention to my bag of groceries. The ice cream was suspiciously soft, but it didn't quite slosh when I shook the container. I threw it in the freezer and hoped for the best. Depositing the rest of the goods on the counter, I washed my hands while scanning the ingredients Monica had set out.

Stocks kissed Monica on the forehead, and snorted at his pathetic excuse for a male ally. "Come on, Brahma, you're embarrassing me. We need to work on those vicious guard dog skills."

The dog reluctantly stood and followed Stocks out the door while Monica joined me at the sink. As we prepared breakfast sandwiches, we watched Stocks and Brahma through the windows. Stocks collected the molding from the truck and took it into the shop as Brahma teetered along behind him, stopping occasionally to sniff and pee on his new territory.

Stocks picked up a small stick and tossed it. Brahma unhurriedly trotted after the stick, and then brought it back, depositing it at Stocks's feet. The resulting grin Stocks flashed us practically split his face in two.

"Just when I think that man can't get any hotter..." Monica fanned herself. "Him playing with a dog shouldn't be sexy, but it is."

"If you want to see the true measure of a man, watch how he treats his inferiors, not his equals," I quoted.

"I like that. Who said it?"

"J. K. Rowling." At the blank stare she gave me, I added, "The creator of Hogwarts?"

Still no recognition in her expression.

"The unbelievably talented and amazing author of Harry Potter. How do you not know who J.K. Rowling is? She's basically a literary god." And, as a child abandoned by my parents, I'd often disappeared from my own shitty reality and into the magical fantasy of witches and wizards, pretending I was a chosen hero, too. Harry Potter and Grandma were probably the only things that kept me going for a while there.

"You're so weird."

She wasn't wrong, so I didn't argue.

Later that evening, we had guests. Havoc, the club's sergeant at arms, was a big black man with arms that had to be twice the diameter of my thighs. His temper was legendary, and like Bull, he drove a tow truck for the club's auto shop. He also ran the club's security. He looked big and scary—always dressed in the club uniform of jeans, T-shirt, and cut—but he was one of the best people I'd ever met. Of course, I was biased since he'd risked himself to save me from Noah Kinlan, and always made me feel welcome and important when I visited the fire station. His wife, Julia, was a gorgeous redhead who owned a small bookstore and dressed like someone who'd never seen a clearance rack in her life. Classy, but never snobby. The two of them couldn't be more different, but the way they looked at each other shattered all stereotypes and preconceived notions about couples.

They brought their baby, Marcus Jr., whose chubby cheeks and dark eyes captivated me from the moment Julia let me pull him out of his carrier. The four other shelter girls who were home crowded me, begging to hold the baby, but I refused to give him up. Turned out Brahma was also selfish. He followed me and Marcus to the rocking chair, sat at my feet, and gave the stink-eye to anyone who dared approach us.

Okay, he really just wagged his tail at them, but I imagined him growling and spitting protectively.

"You sure he's okay around babies?" Havoc asked, watching Brahma like he might have to tackle the dog at any moment.

Brahma laid his head down demurely and kept right on wagging his tail.

I chuckled. "Yeah. He likes kids. His previous owner was a little boy."

Havoc let the matter drop, but he kept one eye on us as he peeled off to talk to Stocks.

During dinner, Stocks and Havoc discussed some home improvement project Havoc was working on while Monica and Julia shared recipes and reviewed newly released novels. Cari, a tall blonde who stayed in the room next to mine, called me out on my hoarder ways and forced me to give up the baby. Marcus spent the meal being passed around the table under Havoc's watchful gaze.

Every time someone shifted the baby, Havoc would call out instructions like, "Watch his head," and, "Be careful of his neck."

"They've got it, baby," Julia kept insisting, patting his hand. Judging by her smile, she didn't mind his protective streak one bit.

After dinner, Havoc rubbed the back of Julia's neck. "How are you feelin'? You tired yet?" Birth complications had forced her into a c-section delivery. It had been six weeks, and she was mostly healed, but Havoc was still in what she referred to as helicopter husband mode.

"No. I'm good."

"You need anything?" His gaze shot to her empty glass. "More water?" Before she could answer, he scooped up the glass and headed for the fridge.

"Relationship goals," Rita, another shelter resident, whispered to me.

I nodded and thought of Bull, feeling the ache in my chest that usually accompanied such thoughts. Bull was protective. He never let me walk home alone, and he never let me pay for anything. I wondered what kind of father and husband he'd be. Did he even want the whole marriage and kids package? We'd covered so much conversational ground as friends, but he always changed the subject when I broached familial topics.

Maybe he just doesn't want a family with me.

The thought punched me in the gut, making my eyes sting and a lump form in my throat. There was undeniable attraction between me and Bull, but he seemed determined not to do anything about it. I needed to break down the walls he was hiding behind and make him surrender his heart to me so we could achieve our own relationship goals.

"You need anything else?" Havoc asked, setting the glass down in front of Julia.

"Actually, I need to use the restroom," she replied, pushing back her chair to stand.

"Want me to go for you?" he asked, rising beside her. Then realizing what he'd said, he amended the statement. "Or at least help you?"

She gave him a patient smile. "Thank you, but I'm fine. Really."

He watched until she stepped out of the kitchen and turned the corner, moving out of his line of sight. The attention he showed her and Marcus was everything I wanted someday.

I just needed Bull to come around.

Meanwhile, I'd suck love and affection from everything around me, especially babies and dogs. "My turn," I demanded, holding my arms out to Rita.

"You had him for like an hour before dinner," she argued.

"Yeah, but he's basically my nephew. Hand him over, or I swear I'll shank you under the table."

"Lily, we talked about this," Monica chided. "All shanking is to be done above the table where I can critique form and strike."

Laughing, Havoc turned to Stocks. "You have your hands full."

"You have no idea. It's like fight club around here," Stocks deadpanned.

Just as I started thinking I'd have to pry Marcus from Rita's cold, dead hands, he messed his pants. Scrunching up her face in disgust, Rita couldn't get him away from her fast enough.

"Want me to get that?" Havoc asked.

I'd grown up babysitting, and had no problem changing diapers. "Nah. I got him. You just relax and enjoy your meal. I'm sure you and Julia don't get to enjoy many warm meals with this little man around."

"Thanks Lily," he said.

"No problem. Just remember, if you ever need a sitter, I'm your girl."

He nodded. "We might take you up on that. I'm going back to work tomorrow, and Julia might need some help over the weekend. You don't start your apprenticeship until Monday, right?"

Confirming, I carried Marcus into the living room and changed his stinky little butt. When I returned, Monica had me bring the baby over so she could get a good look at him.

"Hey Marcus," she cooed, rubbing a finger down the side of his chubby cheek. "I'm your favorite aunt, Moni, and we're gonna be great friends. I'll teach you how to catch frogs, race dirt bikes, fly jets, swear like a pilot, and give your dad all sorts of gray hair."

"Great. Thanks," Havoc grumbled, fighting back a smile. He looked scary, but he was about as vicious as Brahma.

Taming Bull

"Want to hold him?" I asked Monica.

She eyed the baby skeptically. She was kind of weird about babies. Naomi, Monica's best friend, had a toddler named Maya. Monica loved Maya and considered her family, but I rarely saw her hold Maya.

"What's wrong? You scared of babies?" Havoc asked.

"No, I'm not scared of babies," Monica snapped, still watching little Marcus like he was Gizmo, star of an old comedy horror movie. Cute and harmless now, but if she handled him wrong, he'd turn into a gremlin and attack her.

Havoc chuckled. "You sure? You look terrified."

"I'm not scared of babies, per se. I'm scared this whole pregnancy bug could be contagious, and I'm not about that life."

Stocks eyed her. "I don't think pregnancy is contagious, babe."

"That's what the man wants you to think, but you don't know for sure," Monica replied. "The girls all keep catching motherhood like it's the goddamn flu. I ain't catchin' no baby bug, Butter."

She was being ridiculous. "I've been babysitting for more than a decade and haven't gotten pregnant," I said.

"Yeah? Well, you go ahead and take your chances, but I'll be over here livin' my best childless life."

"Oh, come on, Auntie Moni." I leaned closer, practically setting the baby on her lap.

Marcus's eyes drifted to her and he gave her a lopsided smile. He was adorable, and she couldn't help but return the gesture. Recognizing her moment of weakness, I doubled down on my efforts.

"He smiled at you! Look, he likes you." He most likely just had gas, but she didn't need to know that.

"Of course, he likes me. I told you, I'm the cool aunt."

"You sure you're not the chicken aunt?" Havoc asked, goading her.

She scowled at him for a minute before turning on Stocks. "You just gonna let him talk to me like that?"

Stocks threw his hands up in the air. "Do you have any idea how sexy you look with a baby in your arms?"

Her scowl only deepened. "Don't you start in, too. It's bad enough I have my mom beggin' for grandbabies."

"It's your body. Your choice. But you gotta admit, we'd have one hell of a cute baby."

"The cutest." A smile tugged at her lips, but she fought it like a champ. "Okay. Fine. Hand over the little ankle biter."

"Careful with his head and neck," Havoc cautioned.

She snorted. "Oh be quiet, you big lug, I know damn well how to hold a baby."

After the initial awkward handoff, Monica leaned back in her seat, cradling the baby in her arms. As she studied his features, her expression softened. "He's got your big ass forehead, Havoc."

Havoc's eyebrows shot up. "I don't have a big ass forehead."

"Yeah you do. And you passed it along to this poor little man. Thankfully, he's got his mama's cheek bones and eyebrows."

Havoc's lips tugged into a smile. "Yeah."

"His skin is darkening. He was so pale when he was born, but now it's the perfect shade of caramel brown." Her gaze roamed over Stocks and I couldn't help but wonder what was going through her mind. Was she considering what their child would look like? As her attention returned to the baby, emotion flooded her eyes. Her shoulders dropped and she let out a breath. "Fuck."

"What's wrong?" Stocks asked.

She threw her head back and stared at the ceiling. "I think my ovaries just engaged. Dammit, dammit, dammit." Looking back down at Marcus, she added, "Why do you have to be so damn cute?"

Havoc gave her a knowing chuckle. "Changes everything, doesn't it."

"Yeah. I... God, my chest. My fuckin' uterus is screaming. What the hell are you doing to me, little man?"

Havoc's shoulders shook with silent laughter.

Stocks's eyes turned glassy. "You look damn good with a baby in your arms."

"Hush, you. You're not helping." Looking at Havoc, she added, "It's weird. I'd do anything for him. I'd kill anyone who hurt him. What is wrong with me?"

"Just wait until you have one of your own," Havoc said.

Her gaze shot to Stocks. She studied his face for a few heartbeats, and then her eyebrows shot up in question.

Stocks gave her a lopsided grin. "You know I'm game if you are."

She shook her head. "We've gotta be crazy. I'm not supposed to want a baby. I'm supposed to be the cool aunt who spoils the hell out of the club kids *after* they're potty trained and committed to a normal sleeping schedule." She held Marcus up until he was eye level with her. "Will you please do something gross like barf or shit up your back?"

He made the cutest little cooing noise.

"Wail? Or at least fuss a little," she pleaded. "Pretty please? Come on. Wail like a banshee for Auntie."

He gave her another gassy smile.

"Goddammit."

Julia chose that moment to walk back into the dining room. She took one look at Monica and laughed. "Looks like someone has baby fever."

Rita elbowed me. "Hm. You were wrong. Turns out pregnancy is contagious."

7

Bull

"NOW I KNOW what it feels like to be objectified," Tavonte complained, gripping his coffee cup like it was a fucking shield he could use to ward off Ms. Moore's advances. After getting repeatedly accosted during the drive, we'd left the elderly woman in the waiting area of the shop and were working up her invoice. "I need a shower."

"She's a bit handsy," I admitted, trying not to laugh as I pulled up her insurance coverage.

"A bit handsy? That woman's a fuckin' octopus!"

Ms. Moore had spent the entire drive sandwiched between us, with a hand on each of our thighs. No matter how many times we tried to respectfully remove them. She was a lot stronger than she looked, and her vice-like grip was impressive as hell. My favorite moment of the drive was when she'd leaned over to Tavonte and asked him if the rumors about black men were true. He'd choked on air, and then feigned ignorance.

"I don't know which rumors you're talking about, ma'am."

Her gaze dropped to his crotch and she licked her lips. "Oh, I think you do."

Bottling up my laughter took every ounce of willpower I possessed.

She patted Tavonte's leg. "Doesn't matter. This is nice." Sitting back, she seemed reflective. "Reminds me of my old skiing days."

Tavonte's brows drew together and he opened his mouth, no doubt to ask what she meant. Suspecting I knew, and he didn't want to know, I shook my head. That was one disturbing can of worms he wasn't ready to open. He met my gaze and snapped his mouth closed.

Ms. Moore looked pleased as punch as her hands steadily crept up our thighs.

"That woman's not right," Tavonte whispered, sounding scandalized. "She's a grandma. She shouldn't be asking questions about the size of my cock."

"She's just a lonely woman who took advantage of a bad situation."

"You're taking this a little too well. Does this kind of thing happen often around here?"

I applied Ms. Moore's insurance coverage to the invoice and frowned at the difference. "No. But look at us. She obviously has excellent taste."

He snorted. "Hey, what did she mean by that skiing comment? How did being with us remind her of her skiing days?"

I chuckled, preparing to scar Tavonte even further. "We were on either side of her."

He gave me a blank look. The lucky bastard still didn't get it. Ah well, it was my job to enlighten him. Hell, if I was destined to have nightmares about Ms. Moore's advances, so was he.

"You know. Like ski poles," I replied. "One on each side."

His confusion morphed into understanding, and then outrage and disgust. As his eyes widened and his mouth hung open, I had to bite my lip to keep from laughing. He shuddered and threw a not-so-discreet glance over his shoulder to the elderly woman in question. "That's nasty!"

"She's just sowin' her wild oats." I followed his gaze to the waiting area. Wasp had walked in and was talking to Tiffany about a work order. Ms. Moore's jaw was practically brushing against the floor as she watched him in unbridled awe and fiery lust. "Looks like we're safe. She found a new target."

Wasp finished up with the receptionist and stopped in front of Ms. Moore, flashing her a smile. I briefly considered calling him over to warn him, but he was a pro at handling problem customers. I'd seen him smooth talk even the roughest and gruffest, so one sweet but kinky little old lady should be no problem. Besides, the asshole prankster deserved the kind of encounter Ms. Moore's handsy appreciation would provide.

"Hi there. Have you been helped?" he asked.

She nodded and started to stand. Wasp, being the ladies' man he was, offered her his hand. Thanking him, she accepted, allowing him to pull her to her feet. When he released her hand, she clenched his forearm. His gaze drifted down to where they were still connected. Her fingers loosened only enough to slide over his elbow to his bicep. Ms. Moore was clearly into muscles, and our resident power lifter had brawn to spare.

Giving his arm a squeeze, her eyes went wild and she said, "I've never seen a man as big and pretty as you before."

I clamped my lips shut so I wouldn't laugh.

Beside me, Tavonte snickered.

Wasp's glare shot to us, and we both found more interesting things to look at. No need to make fun of one of the three men with the authority to sign my paychecks.

Out of the corner of my eye, I saw Ms. Moore reach for his long, blond hair, but Wasp somehow dodged her advance. Being an amateur body builder, he'd probably evaded his fair share of groping women over the years.

I pointed at the screen, getting Tavonte's attention. "Remember how I was telling you about Morse's software? Well, not only does it give us the customer's towing coverage, but it also runs a soft back-

Taming Bull

ground check." Morse was a goddamn genius. He could get computers to do shit most people would never even imagine. I didn't know how legal his software was, but since we didn't use it for anything nefarious, I couldn't give a shit. "We picked Ms. Moore up a little over three miles outside of what's covered by her policy."

His brows drew together. "So, we charge her for the difference?"

At our usual rates of seventy-five dollars per mile, that'd put her back two-hundred and twenty-five dollars, for the tow alone. And who knew how much her repairs would hike up that cost? "Theoretically, but we have a lot of leeway here." I tapped the financial information on the background check. "She's gonna have a hard enough time paying for the repairs. Adding two hundred dollars for the tow seems cruel."

"So, we don't charge her?"

"Doesn't seem right to. Yes, she's a lonely, sexually frustrated woman who doesn't respect personal space, but she's a single woman on a fixed income." I scrolled down the screen. "And look at that. Her deceased husband was military. I can't charge her."

He eyed me like he was suspicious of my motives.

"Despite what happened between me and Lily this morning, I'm not a complete asshole."

I shouldn't have brought up Lily. All day I'd been trying to forget the way her lip trembled, and her eyes hardened when I refused to talk to her. Mentioning her name conjured her image like I was seeing it again in real time.

"I know you're not, man."

Tavonte's admission healed something inside of me. I shouldn't have cared what he thought of me and the way I'd treated her, but I did. He was a good guy, and I didn't want him to think I was a piece of shit. Hell, I didn't want to *be* a piece of shit. Between a rock and a hard place without many options, I needed all the allies I could get.

Tavonte pointed at the screen. "But you already put in the mileage. How does that work? Do you have to back it out?"

"No. And I wouldn't if I could. We keep clean records. I'll override the difference here." I moved my mouse to the appropriate spot and subtracted the difference to show no balance due. Then I tabbed until I got to where I needed to be. "I'll make a note of why, here. We can write off so much business every year, and Specks is a damn good bookkeeper. When he sees my note, he'll know what to do with it."

Before Tavonte could respond, his cell phone rang. He pulled it out, and concern flashed in his eyes as he glanced at the screen. "It's my mom. She knows I'm shadowing you again today and wouldn't be calling if it wasn't important."

"No problem, brother. Take it."

Tavonte accepted the call with a worried, "Hey, Mom, what's up," as he hurried away from me, giving the call privacy.

Hoping everything was all right with his family, I went back to the screen and finished up Ms. Moore's invoice. Numbers finagled, comments made, I printed the receipt and marched it over to her. Wasp had somehow managed to escape, and was nowhere in sight. Lucky bastard. Making a mental note to beg him for his secrets, I pasted on my most friendly smile and held out the receipt.

"Your insurance covered the tow. As soon as Rabbit diagnoses the problem, he'll let you know the repair cost."

"Rabbit?" Her expression fell. "Not Wasp?"

Aww. She had herself a crush, did she? I was both relieved and strangely disappointed her eyes didn't get all googly when she met my gaze. The appreciation of the opposite sex was always nice for a boost of the ego, regardless of age.

"Yes ma'am. Wasp works in our motorcycle division."

"Oh. I gotta get me one of those."

I didn't know if she was talking about a Wasp or a bike, but I sure as shit didn't encourage her to elaborate. "Can I get you anything while you wait?"

"No, thank you. I'm fine. My daughter's on the way. I gotta warn you now that she's a bit uptight, always afraid I'm gonna get taken advantage of, or some such nonsense. But I know good people when I see 'em." She gave me a conspiratorial grin. "Probably doesn't help that you're all so easy on the eyes, if you know what I mean."

I couldn't have missed her meaning if it was an out of control train and I was tied to the railroad tracks. "Thank you, ma'am. We try to stay in shape."

"Well, let me tell you, I, for one, sure do appreciate it."

I coughed back a laugh. "Rabbit'll be with you when he finishes the diagnostics. Please help yourself to any refreshments," I pointed at the fridge and coffee area, "and let Tiffany know if you need anything."

Tiffany waved and smiled, making her presence known.

As I started to walk away, Ms. Moore grabbed my arm. Thinking I was going to have to scrape her off again, I was surprised to see genuine appreciation—and not lust—in her eyes. "I know the towing package on my insurance didn't cover the full tow here, young man. My daughter ran the mileage and she warned me I'd have to pay for a little over three miles. You lot took good care of my friend, Niles Fredrickson. He said you look out for veterans and their spouses."

I remembered Mr. Fredrickson. He was a cantankerous old Marine. Looking to save some money, he'd let his grandson change the timing belt on his 4-Runner. The kid was only trying to help, but he'd botched up the install, resulting in bent intake valves in the cylinder head. Mr. Fredrickson had recently had a triple-bypass surgery, and was dangerously close to working himself into another heart attack in our shop, complaining about the VA's handling of the surgery. Rabbit had taken pity on the old bastard and had only charged him for parts, donating his time and labor, insisting it was the least he could do.

We didn't advertise our altruism, and we didn't give discounts for the recognition. Vets gave a lot for their country, and we preferred to let them keep their pride. I didn't know how to respond to Ms. Moore's assessment, so I nodded, silently confirming that we took care of our own.

She grasped my hand. "Thank you," she said, her eyes brimming with gratitude. "You do a really good thing here."

My chest swelled with pride. I'd fucked up a lot of things in my life. Kicked out of the Navy, rocky relationship with my family, I'd blown my friendship with Lily and had no idea what to do about the situation we were in. Despite it all, I could do this one nice thing for a fellow serviceman's widow. It felt damn good. Even choked me up a little. Ducking my head, I swallowed past the emotion in my throat and replied, "My pleasure, ma'am."

When Tavonte got off his phone, he looked a little frazzled. Another tow request had been made, so he followed me to the truck and climbed into the passenger's seat. I wanted to know what was bothering him, but he apparently had some research to do. As I drove, he mashed buttons on his phone. After a while, he pulled out his wallet and entered his credit card information before pocketing his things and taking a deep breath.

"Everything okay?" I asked.

"Nope. I gotta go home," he said.

I wasn't expecting that. "Home? As in back to Nashville?" I asked. Then, because he looked so damn stressed out, I did my best to lighten the mood. "Damn. Ms. Moore really scared you off, didn't she?"

He barked out a laugh and shook his head. "If only. Unfortunately, this is nuthin' as simple as customer sexual harassment. My little sister's gotten herself in with a bad crowd, and mom's worried about her. I gotta go see what kind of shit she's stepped in and get her cleaned up."

"Damn, brother, I'm sorry to hear it. Sure hope she and your mom are okay."

"Yeah. Me too. Thanks, man."

"When are you leaving?"

"Just booked a flight for the day after tomorrow. Mom sounded scared. I... Fuck. I'm gonna kill Kiana for putting her through this."

"Think you'll be back?"

He toyed with his phone for a moment before shaking his head. "No. I really respect what you guys are doing here. Helping veterans... acting as a landing pad when guys get out of the service... It's a fuckin' noble cause, man. I want to be part of it, but although I'm down with what you're doin', I can't shake this feeling that I'm not supposed to stay. There's something out there for me, but this isn't it. And I don't want to stay here and miss out on whatever's out there waiting for me."

Tavonte's hesitancy to commit to the club suddenly made sense. For two weeks now, he'd been shadowing me at work. He always engaged in conversation with the brothers. His suggestions were golden, and he fit right in, but he seemed hesitant to lay down roots. I wondered if Link knew he wouldn't stay, and that's why he had him riding with me instead of hanging out in the shop with the rest of the mechanics. He'd become a friend, and I was bummed he wouldn't be sticking around.

Still, I understood him completely. That was exactly the way I'd felt before I left for the Navy. "Be careful, man. Sometimes you go lookin', and you lose more than you gain."

He frowned at me. "You and I both know you would have suffocated in some small Texas town."

I wasn't ready for that kind of introspection, so I lightened the conversation. "Well, this sucks. Here I thought we were gonna bond as Ms. Moore's ski poles."

Tavonte shuddered, then dropped his head. His shoulders shook as he chuckled. "Sick, man. I can't believe you put that visual in my head. Again."

"Consider it a parting gift. You're welcome. Have you let Link know you're leaving yet?"

He flipped his phone in the air and caught it. "No. I should probably get on that, huh?"

"Yeah. He'll want everyone to gather and send you off."

Tavonte cocked his head to the side and gave me a brow lift. "Why? It's not like I joined or anything. The club doesn't owe me shit."

"Be that as it may, you gave ten years of your life in service to this country, and now you're rushing off to help your mom and sister. You may not be a Dead President, but you're sure as hell one of us."

He gave me a lopsided grin before hitting a button on his phone and holding it to his ear. "Thanks, brother. I can't stay, but I'm sure as shit glad I stopped here."

I clapped him on the shoulder. "Yeah. Me too."

8

Bull

I FIGURED LILY would be at Tavonte's going away party, but I was in no way prepared for the actual sight of her. It felt like coming across a bottle of water after a long run through the desert in full gear. But she was still just out of my reach. Wearing distressed skinny jeans, a tight black Harley shirt, and black knee-high boots, she looked like a biker's wet dream: sexy, soft, and a little badass. Her long, brown hair was down in big, soft curls that made me want to run them through my fingers to feel the silky strands. Her eyes and lips were made up to look even bigger and more seductive than usual. It was like every time I saw her, she got hotter.

One of these days, she was going to burn up my retinas.

Her tight-ass T-shirt left little to the imagination. Plain as day, the outline of her breasts promised one hell of a good time. She'd filled out some since I'd first met her, and her more pronounced curves were tempting as fuck. Her slender waist led into hips I'd love to grip as I took her from behind. She spun around to talk to Carly, and I got an eyeful of the most perfect ass Seattle had to offer.

God, the way it strained the taut fabric of her jeans made me wish I was denim. The memory of her licking her beer bottle popped into my mind and my cock strained painfully against the back of my zipper.

Fuck!

Adjusting my erection, I forced myself to remember that this was Lily I was eye-fucking. Shit would never work between us, so I had to play it cool. I had no business looking at her like she was a goddamn warm apple pie I wanted to eat. Or stick my dick in. Maybe lick then fuck.

Get it together, Roberts, she's like a sister to you.

Only, she wasn't. Not at all. That lie hadn't worked on Lily, and it sure as shit wasn't working on me. I had to force myself to look away. If I didn't, I'd walk over there, grab her hand, and tow her fine ass up to my room. And then where would we be? Would I really throw away our friendship just to get my dick wet?

Maybe.

It wasn't like we were on the friendliest of terms now, so what did I have to lose.

Everything.

The entire club would hate me if I hurt Lily. Hell, I'd hate myself.

That sobering promise of self-loathing gave me the strength I needed to pull my gaze away from her enticing body. Still keeping her in my peripheral—so I could continue to check her out without being tempted to jump her bones—I made small talk with some of the brothers around me. But I honestly couldn't remember a damn thing that was said. All I could think about was Lily. How she looked. What she'd feel like, writhing under me. What kind of noises she'd make when she came.

The way the people of my hometown would look at her if I ever brought her home.

Shit!

"When are you gonna man up and talk to her?" Tavonte asked, pulling me out of my fucked-up musings.

I turned to face him, effectively losing sight of the object of my obsession. "What the fuck are you talking about?"

He chuckled and handed me a beer. It was my fourth in the last two hours, and although I was far from drunk, the effects were making their presence known. Which was probably why I was having such a hard time resisting Lily. I didn't need a fourth beer, but I couldn't handle being sober with her in the room, either.

"You're not that slick, Bull. You've been low-key creepin' on Lily all night."

He'd caught me. There was no use denying it, so I came clean-ish. "I'm not creeping. I'm lookin' out for her."

His arched eyebrow told me he wasn't buying my bullshit.

"She's a lightweight, and I saw her take a couple shots of Fireball." Two shots, and she'd had at least as many bottles of water. She was probably more sober than I was. "I'm making sure none of these motherfuckers take advantage of her while she's drinkin'." I was so full of shit my grey eyes had probably turned brown. I was the only thing Lily had to fear in this club, and we both knew it.

"Keep tellin' yourself that, bro."

"I will, thanks." I already had a ticket to hell for all the shit I wanted to do to Lily's body, might as well upgrade my seat with more lies. "It's the goddamn truth."

"Cut the shit and follow me." Tavonte started walking.

Feeling particularly rebellious, I decided I didn't want to follow him. He seemed to be in another bossy, preachy phase, and was looking for a goddamn soapbox. I was in no mood to be lectured about wasting chocolate cake. He didn't know my life. He didn't have all the details, and he sure as hell couldn't judge me. Besides, the asshole was leaving tomorrow. I could slip away, avoid him for the rest of the night, and not have to face whatever music he was determined to play for me.

He's a friend. Don't be a chickenshit, Roberts.

Truth was, I'd miss his meddling ways. I didn't want to brush him off before he left. I watched his back for only a moment more before guilt and curiosity finally got the best of me. I padded after him, weaving through bikers, ol' ladies, and club whores until we got to the empty sofa in the corner of the common area. We were still part of the party, but far enough away from the group to hold a private conversation.

He sat on the patched up old sofa and gestured for me to do the same. When I did, he put his elbows on his knees and leaned forward, giving me his full attention.

"Before I leave, I want you to do something for me," he said.

I had the distinct feeling I wouldn't like his request, so I requested more details before committing. "What do you want me to do?"

"Be straight with me. Tell me what's really going on between you and Lily?"

What was he, Dr. Phill? "Why?"

"Why not?" he fired back.

"Because it's none of your damn business. Why do you even care?"

He shook his head and sat back. "Good question. I don't even know. Maybe it's because I see you doin' all this shit for other people and I think you're a good guy who deserves to be happy."

Needing a moment to digest his assessment, I looked away. My gaze unconsciously sought out Lily. She had Tap's daughter on her hip and was swaying to the music. She looked like a fucking angel, and I couldn't tear my attention away. She must have sensed me watching her, because she met my gaze and gave me a tentative smile. She should be pissed at me for the way I'd treated her when she brought me donuts, but that smile sang of grace and mercy.

I didn't deserve either.

I dropped my gaze to my hands.

Tavonte chuckled. "Look, it's obvious you two are into each other. You treated her like shit at the shop yesterday, but I know you're not an asshole, so I'm guessing there's more to the story. You don't owe me an explanation, but maybe you need someone to talk to. I don't got a dog in this fight, and my ass is heading to Nashville tomorrow. If you need to get something off your chest... this is your golden opportunity."

Tavonte made a lot of sense. The attraction I felt toward Lily only seemed to be getting worse, and I wasn't sure how long I could continue to fight it. I missed her companionship. But I was terrified of the way she kept pushing me for more. What if I gave in and we did something we'd both regret?

"Come on, man. Talk to me. What do you have to lose?"

Nothing. I'd already lost everything. I sat back and tugged at a small hole in my jeans. "Since you're from the city, I feel like I need to start by explaining my hometown. It's small. Really small. When I got in trouble at school for rubbing Robbie Grindle's face in the dirt, my mom knew before I got home. Not because my teacher called her, but because Jessie Stuart told her mom who called the entire prayer circle to pray for my badass little self."

Tavonte chuckled. "Okay, that's small."

"Yeah. Everyone knows everyone. Anyway, my mom's best friend had a daughter my age. Amber." If I closed my eyes, I could still see her sitting at her desk in kindergarten. Larry Frampton had put a frog on her chair, and I'd cleaned his clock for it. Larry and I had just gotten told to go to the principal's office when Amber grabbed my arm. She smiled up at me, and I knew right then my destiny was set. I knew I was going to marry that girl.

"We grew up together. She was my best friend before I even knew what friends were. She was shy and sweet, and I was always there to protect her. I don't even remember when we started dating. It was natural progression, or some shit like that. After high school, I bought her a ring and promised to marry her. But first, I needed to put in my time in the service. It was all good, because Amber had dreams of her own. She wanted to go to school and get certified to work with special needs kids. We were planning to get hitched after my four years in the Navy."

Because I was single and in Seattle, it was clear my story didn't have a happy ending. Tavonte's brow furrowed and he steepled his fingers. "What happened?"

"While Amber was away at college, she... she had a run-in with some asshole. She reported it, but he was a privileged little fuck, and nobody believed her."

"What kind of run-in?"

I knew I was being evasive, but there were some details I couldn't even admit to myself. Still, this was my chance to get it all off my chest, and I needed to be transparent. "She was raped."

He sucked in a breath. "I see. You said nobody believed her. What about you? You believed her, right?"

I felt the familiar stab in my chest when I thought about Amber. I had so many questions about her rape, but answers would forever be out of my reach. "She didn't tell me," I admitted.

Tavonte's eyes widened with shock.

It was an appropriate response. Sure, I wasn't much of a talker, but I was a damn good listener. She should have trusted me with the truth. I'd spent so many nights lying awake and wondering what had happened. Was she at a party? Was she drinking? Did she feel guilty? Was she afraid she'd led him on? She could have been honest with me and I wouldn't have given a single fuck about the circumstances. I sure as hell wouldn't have blamed her. I would have wanted to kill the fucker, but I also would have reassured her. I would have fought for her. I would have made calls and jumped through hoops. I would have found that piece of shit and no amount of his daddy's dollars could have kept me from nailing his balls to the wall. I would have found a way to protect her from whatever hell he'd put her through.

But in the end, she didn't tell me.

He'd taken her virginity and she'd taken her life, both of which were promised to me, and I was left with nothing. Not even an explanation.

"She didn't tell you?" Tavonte asked, drawing me out of my painful memories. "Why not? How'd you find out?"

"She... She committed suicide, Tay. I found out after she was dead."

His jaw dropped.

Pain stabbed at me. Years had passed, and the hurt had dulled, but the fact she hadn't trusted me to love her through everything still fucking burned. What kind of man doesn't protect his woman?

Me.

I hadn't.

And she hadn't trusted me to.

"Fuck," Tavonte finally muttered.

The expression seemed woefully inadequate, but English didn't offer a better alternative. "Yeah. Fuck."

"I'm sorry, man. I just..." He ran a hand over his head. "Holy shit."

Tavonte looked like he needed a minute. I could relate. It had been years, and I still couldn't process what had happened. Giving him time, I drained my beer, and then went in search of another. We'd need it. Hell, there probably wasn't enough beer in Seattle to help me get through the rest of the story. Still, there was something therapeutic about laying it all out there like this. I was surprised to find that the edge had blunted. The past wasn't cutting me as deeply anymore.

By the time I returned with our drinks, Tavonte had gotten his expression under control. Shock and awe had been replaced with a steely determination to understand my plight. "I can't even imagine what you must have gone through. Is this why you won't give Lily a chance? You're afraid of something like this happening again?"

If only it was that simple. I plopped his beer on the coffee table in front of him and sat with mine in hand. "No. You ready for the rest of the story?"

His eyebrows drew together. "There's more?"

"Yep. You can tap out now if you need to."

Looking like he wanted to, he exchanged his empty bottle for the full one and took a long pull. Squaring his shoulders like he was climbing back into the ring after having his bell rung, he said, "Okay. I'm ready. Bring it."

"The night Havoc met Lily, she was..." Anger gripped me, squeezing my tongue and making it difficult to speak. I swallowed past it and tried again. "She was being attacked. Havoc beat the shit out of her attacker, but not before..." God, why was this so fucking hard to say?

Understanding was written all over Tavonte's face. "She was raped, too?"

I nodded, grateful he'd saved me the trouble of admitting it aloud. "It's not as rare as you'd think. Nearly one in five American women is the victim of rape or attempted rape. That shit happens far too often."

"Wow. I didn't realize it was that common. That's fuckin' awful." He sipped from his bottle.

"Yeah. Lily's family isn't much to speak of, and she moved to Seattle when her grandma died. She wanted to get as far away from Georgia as possible. After the attack, the club kinda adopted her." I remembered the night she came to the fire station, looking scared, alone, and so much like my dead fiancée, it hurt to look at her.

"That's good. If those statistics of yours are right, sounds like a club of overprotective veteran biker guardians is what every girl needs."

I chuckled. "Yeah. She's been through a lot. Nobody wants to see her get hurt."

"And you think you'll hurt her?" Tavonte asked.

"Not intentionally, no. But there's a lot of shit I can't give her. Shit she needs." I pulled out my wallet and flipped it open to Amber's senior picture. God, she was gorgeous, and if I didn't know better, I'd swear I was looking at a picture of Lily. Holding open my wallet, I showed the portrait to Tavonte.

"Lily?" he asked. His gaze immediately sought her out across the room.

"No. That's Amber."

His eyebrows jumped up his forehead. "Your... ex?"

"Yep."

"What the fuck?"

"Exactly. If Lily and I get together, it'll be the real deal. It'll be forever. She needs a family. She deserves to marry someone who can give her one. I can't. My parents are best friends with Amber's, and if I bring home Amber's doppelganger... how fucked up would that be?"

"Shit, man." Tavonte scratched at the stubble on his jaw. "I hear ya, loud and clear."

Feeling vindicated for the way I'd pushed Lily away, I straightened. "Thank you. Now you see why I gotta be an asshole. She wants more than friendship, and this thing between us... it'll never work."

He met my gaze. "You know about my dad... about how he died in the service. What you don't know is that my stepdad did, too. Mack was a Seal. And coincidentally, a biker. He was a good guy, and the best damn stand-in dad I could have asked for. Then one day, he went out to shoot hoops with a buddy. He got winded and said he needed a minute. He sat down, and he never got back up. Died right there on the court. Turned out he had a heart defect no examination had found. His death about destroyed my mom. My sister was just a baby, and if Mom didn't have us to take care of, I think she would have given up."

Wondering what his story had to do with my situation, I frowned. "I'm sorry, brother."

He shrugged. "It's crazy, you know. Years later, right before I went into the service, I asked mom about her husbands. I wanted to know if it was worth it."

"Worth what?" I asked.

"She was married to each of them for such a short time, I wondered if the love they shared—the good times—if it was worth all the pain."

"What'd she say?" I asked, suddenly needing to know.

"She looked me in the eye and said, 'Yes. There's nuthin' in the world like knowin' you're loved. If I had to do it all again, I would. But I sure as hell wouldn't have made Mack wait so long. I would have married that man the first time he asked, and to hell with anyone's opinion about how long a widow should wait.'"

I stared at him, wondering what to say.

"So, no. I don't see why you and Lily shouldn't be together. I see a good man who's making a misguided decision for a woman who has her own mind and should be able to make her own damn decision. You wanna know what Lily really deserves? She deserves a choice. It's kinda ironic how pissed you are at Amber for not coming to you with her life changing, devastating news, when you're doing the same thing to Lily."

He was right.

I felt the truth of his words, and they knocked the goddamn wind out of me.

"Don't make the same mistake Amber made," Tavonte said, standing. "Tell her. As my mom would advise you, tell her now. Your ass isn't promised tomorrow."

9

Lily

I HAVE A dog. *I'm surrounded by babies and friends. I'm beginning an awesome apprenticeship soon. My life is amazing. And full.* Hell, it's so complete it's practically a new game of Jenga. All my pieces are together, and nothing's in danger of going sideways. *I have everything I need.*

A man? I scoffed at the idea.

I don't need a man. I've got this. I'm a fuckin' boss.

You know what? I'll be my own man.

That probably wasn't a thing, but I was going with it. Affirmations stuck on repeat in my head, I waded through happy couples and competed for the affection of their children. I wasn't sure how many times I needed to lie to myself before I brainwashed my subconscious into not constantly seeking out Bull, but I had to be making progress. I'd turned avoiding him into a goal, and I crushed goals. I made goals my bitches.

My gaze unconsciously landed on the source of my torment, and I wanted to kick my own ass.

Dammit! I was doing so good.

Since Hailey was on my hip, dancing with me to the music, I couldn't very well beat my head against the wall, but I was tempted. Still, I needed to keep moving so the five-year-old little ball of energy would forget how badly she wanted to play with Trent. Unfortunately, he sprinted by, flying a plastic dragon over his head. It was too much temptation for her to handle. She tugged on my shirt and asked to be put down. Understanding how she felt—it was taking everything within me not to chase after my own best friend—I briefly considered pretending I couldn't hear her over the music and surrounding conversations. I'd be doing the girl a favor. If she learned to deny herself now, it'd save her so much trouble in the long run.

But, why delay the inevitable?

I set her down and she scurried off in the direction Trent had disappeared in, without so much as a goodbye. Trying not to feel completely abandoned, I refocused on the many blessings of my life. Grandma used to say gratitude was the key to happiness. I had more to be grateful for now, than ever. Joy should be oozing out of my goddamn pores like oil and dead skin cells. Contentment should be radiating from me like fucking sunshine.

So, why did I feel so gloomy?

My gaze shot to Bull.

Dammit!

Maybe I needed a rubber band around my wrist that I could snap every time I saw him. Or possibly a shock collar? Hot sauce was another option, but it wouldn't work for me. When I was still sucking my thumb past my toddler days, Grandma used to dip it in Tapatio, thinking the heat would cure me of the habit. Instead, I'd discovered my love for spice. A rubber band or a shock collar would probably just push me into masochism.

How did I get this fucked up?

Bull was once again in my sights.

I'd most likely have to gouge out my eyeballs to break this addiction.

It frustrated me to no end that he wouldn't talk to me. Couldn't he see how perfect we were together? They say friends make the best lovers, and he'd been my best friend for two years. How could he cut me off like this?

Wasn't he lonely without me?

Stop, Lily. That way lies madness.

I missed my grandma. My hand instinctively reached for the necklace she'd given me, as if touching it could conjure up the wisdom of a woman who'd been gone for almost three years. If she were alive today, she'd tell me to keep on counting my blessings.

Then again, maybe not.

Grandma's advice was rarely what I expected, but always what I needed. And I didn't need to count my blessings, because I wasn't short on gratitude. Hell, I had gratitude up the wazoo.

What I didn't have, was Bull.

"How are you, Lil?" Carly asked, interrupting my introspection. Out of all the ol' ladies, Carly was the closest to my age, but being a single mom meant she was lightyears ahead in maturity. To be honest, I felt a tad intimidated by how much she'd accomplished in her life. We'd both fled to Seattle to start a new life, but where I had struggled just to pull myself up by my bootstraps, Carly had done it with a kid holding her down and a stalker on her tail. She was tough and resilient, and I kind of wanted to be her when I grew up.

Not wanting her to worry about me and my non-existent love life, I pasted on a smile. "I'm good. How are you?"

The concern in her eyes said she could see right through me. "You sure?"

"Yeah. Totally. I'm great." My gaze dropped down to her belly where the cutest little baby bump was beginning to show. I wasn't sure if I'd been too upset to notice the bump when Carly drove me home, or if she'd just started showing in the past two weeks, but the evidence was definitely there now. Monica had been right to fear the contagion of pregnancy, because babies were popping up all over this club. "Stocks said Wasp announced your pregnancy during church. Congratulations."

Carly was a natural girl-next-door beauty, but right then, her smile was stunning. It lit up her entire being as her hand landed on her belly. I'd seen glowing pregnant women before, but this was different. More. She freaking radiated.

"Thank you," she said. "We didn't want to tell anyone until after the first trimester, but it looks like we barely passed that hurdle in time. I'm much bigger than I was with Trent at this stage, and I'm not sure how much longer we could have kept *this* a secret."

"Well, you look gorgeous. Is Trent happy about becoming a big brother?"

"Thank you." Carly's gaze cut to where her seven-year-old son was playing with Hailey. "And he's over the moon about it. I don't even think he cares whether it's a girl or a boy. He's just excited to have another friend to play with. It's crazy how well he's thrived here at the club. Thinking back to how awful things were when I first moved to Seattle... I... it's overwhelming. I don't know what I would have done if Flint hadn't taken a chance and offered me a job at the Copper Penny." Her eyes welled up and two fat tears rolled down her cheeks. Surprise raised her eyebrows, and then she laughed and brushed the moisture away. "Sorry. Pregnancy hormones. They're kinda stupid. The waterworks randomly go off and I don't know why. I'm not even sad."

No, she sure wasn't. It was like Carly had her own joyful atmosphere, and I felt lighter and more at ease just being near her. "Are you still working?" I hadn't been back to the bar since my fight with Bull, so I wasn't sure.

"I just gave notice. Flint grumbled and threatened to kick Wasp's ass for knocking up his best bartender, but I know that sweet ol' grouch is secretly happy for us. I *could* work up until my due date—I did with Trent—but Wasp won't hear none of it. I swear, that man would like nothing more than to cover me in bubble wrap and stick me on the sofa with my feet hiked up for the next six months."

Carly didn't see Wasp sneaking up behind her, but I did. I smiled as he wrapped his arms around her, settling his hands on her belly. "Now, that's not true, Dove. I'd rather have you in my bed, naked, with your feet hiked up for the next thirty years or so."

Chiding him for being an overprotective, horny brute, she tried to slide out of his grip, but Wasp tickled her until she stopped squirming. Giving up, she leaned against him. He slid her hair behind one shoulder and bent to nuzzle her neck.

Loneliness hollowed me out again. Not wanting to torture myself by sticking around to watch the lovebirds, I prepared to make my escape. But Wasp pinned me in place with a look. "Hey, Lil, how are you?" he asked.

What was it with these people and all their concerns about my well-being? Dodging their questions was getting old. "I'm good. Carly's glowing."

He grinned. "Oh, I know she is. She looks damn good pregnant, doesn't she?"

Carly blushed.

"Yep. She's gorgeous."

Wasp's smile was redirected over my head. "Bull," he said with a nod. "Hey brother."

Bull?

My heart sped up and goosebumps rose across my arms at his presence. I could feel him behind me for fuck's sake! Forcing myself to stay put—and not turn around and throw myself at him—I held my breath and waited.

"Hey, Wasp. Carly," Bull said. "Mind if I steal Lily for a few minutes?"

He wanted to steal me, and by God, I wanted to be stolen. But something was happening to Carly. It was like she started morphing before my very eyes. Her smile vanished, stealing away her ethereal radiance. Eyes narrowed to slits and burning with hellfire, she ripped free of Wasp's arms and took an aggressive step forward. She'd gone from glowing to raging in one-point-three seconds flat, and I was so damned shocked, I didn't know what to do.

"That depends. Exactly how big of an asshole are you planning to be to her?" Her voice reminded me of Sigourney Weaver's demon possessed character in *The Ghostbusters*. I fully expected the next words out of her mouth to be, *'Are you the Keymaster?'*

If Bull turned and ran for his life, I wouldn't have blamed him one bit. Instead, he stepped beside me and grabbed my hand, lacing our fingers. Not expecting the contact, I hadn't braced for it, and I felt everything. The callouses on his hands rubbed against mine as little sparks shot up my arm, zinging me right in the heart. If he kept affecting me like this, I'd need a defibrillator soon.

Then again, maybe a pair of heart paddles would shock some sense into me.

The man had sister-zoned me, brushed me off, and treated me like shit. I should be angrily washing my hands of him, but instead, it was all I could do not to close the rest of the distance between us and lay my head on his shoulder. I hated myself for the way I reacted to his touch, but I was powerless to resist his pull.

"No, ma'am. Being an asshole to Lily is not my goal," Bull said.

Carly's hand sprung up and her index finger landed smack in the center of Bull's chest, hard enough to bruise. "Don't you try that charming southern shit on me. It might not be your goal, but it better not be an unfortunate side effect, either. Hurt her, and you'll have me to deal with. I'll find you, and I will destroy you. *Capisce?*"

Now, I couldn't tell if Carly was channeling Liam Neeson from *Taken* or auditioning for the next *Godfather* movie, but I was sure glad her animosity wasn't directed at me. It shouldn't surprise anyone that Wasp's spawn had her acting all whack-a-doodle, but this behavior was so out of character, I was concerned she might need an exorcism.

Bull winced, but didn't back down. Letting her drill his breastbone with her index finger, he released my hand and slowly raised both of his in surrender. "Yes, ma'am. I hear ya loud and clear."

I simultaneously missed his touch and hated myself for being so damn needy.

Carly's gaze shifted to me, and a little of the fire and brimstone ebbed from her eyes. "You don't have to go with him if you don't want to."

I'd never admit it aloud, but watching her go from girl-next-door to demonic mobster to defend me was nice. Her protective—albeit concerning—behavior reminded me that although Grandma was gone, several strong, amazing women had my back. I wasn't alone anymore. I hadn't been for quite some time. Regardless, I didn't need Carly, or anyone else, fighting my battles. "It's okay; I want to talk to him." I gave Bull a little side-eye action, letting him know he wasn't out of the woods yet. "We're overdue for a conversation. Thank you, Carly, but I'll be fine."

Reaching out, she grabbed my hand and gave it a squeeze of solidarity. "You sure?"

I nodded.

"Okay, but if you need me, I'll be right here." She cast another glare in Bull's direction. "And you... you remember what I said, buck-o."

Wasp put his hands on Carly's shoulders and reeled her in. As usual, his eyes were full of mischief, and a lopsided smirk tugged at his lips. "Come on, my little firecracker. As hot as it is to see you all worked up like this, I don't think it's good for the baby. Let's go sit you down, put your feet up, and see if we can't lower your blood pressure a little."

Carly hesitantly let her husband lead her off. Once they were out of ear shot, I turned toward Bull and waited.

"Carly used to like me," he said, still staring after the couple with his sad bullmastiff eyes.

"I'm sure she will again. She's protective, and well... pregnant."

"You mean terrifying."

I chuckled. He wasn't wrong.

"I don't think I'll be hittin' the Copper Penny again until after she goes on maternity leave."

"That's probably wise. She might try to sacrifice you to Zuul."

He turned his attention back to me, and I could see the shadow of my long-lost friend in the quirk of his lips. "You were thinking Ghostbusters, too?"

It was almost like I had my friend back. Grinning, I replied, "Of course. That was classic Gatekeeper. If I could figure out how she channeled demigods like that, I could make Burger Villa serve breakfast again."

His eyes widened. "Burger Villa stopped serving breakfast?" At my nod, he added, "But what about their amazing sausage bagels?"

Glad someone had finally validated my previous outrage on the subject, I shouted, "Yes! Thank you."

"Why would they do that? That's horrible."

This was exactly why I needed Bull in my life. He got me, like nobody else in the world. We stood in silence for a moment, just staring at one another. I wondered if he was thinking the same thing. Maybe not. Before our last fight, I would have sworn I knew more about him than anybody, but he'd never told me about Amber. I couldn't help but wonder what other big secrets my bestie was hiding from me.

Also, I felt Amber's presence. She'd been along for the ride the whole time, like some third wheel I hadn't known was there, but kept pulling us out of alignment every time we made progress. If we had any chance of moving forward, we needed to come up with a plan to cut her loose.

"We need to talk. Wanna go somewhere quiet?" Bull asked.

Exactly what I was thinking. He often said I wore my thoughts and opinions all over my face, but his ability to read me could be downright creepy sometimes. I nodded. Butterflies erupted in my stomach, and my heart leapt at the realization I'd finally get a chance to bridge this chasm between us. Knowing I wouldn't have to plead my case in front of the entire club only sweetened the deal. "Sure."

Before he could change his mind, I grabbed his hand. Although he'd slid his into mine earlier, I half expected him to pull away, but he didn't. If we were going to finally talk about this thing between us, I wanted that discussion to take place someplace with a door we could lock. A bed would be nice, too, in case Bull was ready to admit to how wrong he'd been and beg me to forever be his. Preferably with his face between my thighs.

Hey, a girl can dream.

Scurrying up the stairs while trying to tamp down my excitement and force my feet to slow, I tugged him along. I'd never been in Bull's room before. Sure, I'd tried to weasel my way in a few times, but he was kind of old fashioned, and didn't want people sullying my good name. Or maybe his? It was part of that southern charm Carly had mentioned. As far as I knew, no girls but Lacy had ever seen the inside of his room, and she wasn't in there long enough to even tell me what it looked like. Regardless, I knew right where it was. I marched us in and closed the door before he could come to his senses and kick me out. Hitting the light switch, I spun around to take it all in.

The room was bare.

There was no overhead light. Instead, the switch had turned on a small lamp on Bull's dresser. It cast the sparse room in a dim glow. I don't know what I'd been expecting, but the only personal touch Bull had added was a framed picture of his family that perched on the nightstand. His bed was made and tucked tight, complete with hospital corners. Everything was clean, in its place, and completely devoid of character. His sliding closet door was closed, but I'd bet both my big toes his clothes were hung, all facing the same direction, and in order by color. As if he owned anything other than black T-shirts and jeans. I'd never seen the inside of a military barracks building, but if there were individual sleeping rooms, they'd look exactly like this.

Temporary.

Borderline sterile.

It made me strangely sad. Bull had been with the Dead Presidents for two years, and as far as I knew, he had no intention of leaving. So, why was his place so barren?

"Where's all your stuff?" I asked.

He swept a hand around to encompass the entirety of the room. "You're lookin' at it. I don't need much."

But what about the belongings he'd acquired growing up? Before Stocks and Monica had taken over the shelter, I kept all my worldly possessions in two bags that I could easily carry, knowing that at any moment I might have to find somewhere else to crash, but Bull has never known the uncertainty of being homeless. He went from his childhood home, to the Navy, to the fire station. He could have had his belongings shipped up from Texas, but maybe he didn't want any reminders of his old life.

While I pondered his motives, he wandered over and sat on the bed absentmindedly.

Wanting to comfort him, to let him know I understood the pain and loneliness of an empty room, I locked the door.

His brows rose. Gaze drifting from the doorknob, to me, and then to the bed, he sprang to his feet. The sight was comical, but I forced myself not to laugh. "We... we shouldn't be in here," he stammered.

I leveled a stare at him. "Yes, we should. We're both adults, and we need to have an uninterrupted conversation." And if our chat happened to end up horizontal, I, for one, wouldn't object. And I sure as hell didn't want anyone busting in to stop us.

His nod was skeptical at best, but he gestured toward the sofa. "Have a seat."

The bed looked a hell of a lot more comfortable, but just

making it into his room seemed like a big step. I relented and sat on the sofa, hoping to make him more at ease.

Bull joined me, sitting at the opposite end, as far away as he could get. Since it was a loveseat, and he was tall, he couldn't keep our knees from touching. "I'm... I'm sorry about the way I treated you at the shop," he started.

His apology was unexpected, and I shrugged it off. "That's okay."

"No, it's not. I wasn't trying to hurt you, Lily, and I'm sorry if I did. There's... I... I know you want more from me than friendship, and I can't give you what you're lookin' for. I thought it would be easier to go our separate ways."

His admission felt like a kick to my sternum. I wasn't even a hundred percent sure what a sternum was, but whatever it was reeled from his blow. "Easier for who?" I asked. When he didn't answer, I continued. "Because I gotta be straight with you, Bull, I hate the way we're avoiding each other right now. This isn't easier. I miss you. I can't tell you how many times I've picked up my phone to text or call you, only to remember that your ass won't respond. It sucks. I feel like I've lost my best friend, and I don't understand why. Don't you miss me at all?"

His frown deepened. "Yes. Of course I do."

I froze, surprised he'd actually admitted it. "Then why are you pushing me away?"

He looked away, and his chest rose and fell with a deep breath. "There's a lot of shit you don't know about me."

"Then tell me!" I pleaded. "My God, Bull, I've never once judged you. You can tell me anything. That's what I thought we were doing with this whole friendship thing. Everyone else thinks I'm an orphan. You're the only one who knows my asshole parental units left me with my grandma and split. I trusted you with all my secrets. Why won't you trust me with yours?"

His shoulders fell in defeat. "Because I'm an idiot, and I thought keeping it to myself would make shit easier."

"If you push me away again, I swear I will buy every snake in Seattle and put them in your bed." Since he was terrified of snakes, it was a solid threat.

"You wouldn't."

"Test me, motherfucker."

We locked gazes. I studied the grey of his eyes, refusing to so much as blink. Finally, he smirked and broke. "I can't believe how much I missed this shit."

He did miss me. I knew it. Doing my best not to gloat, I channeled Carly and said, "Spill, buck-o."

"Fine." He sat back. "Before I left the Navy, I was engaged."

His admission somehow managed to suck all the oxygen from the room. I'd known about Amber, but engaged? That was new and unwelcome information.

"Her name was Amber, and I'd grown up with her."

"Did you love her?" I blurted out, unable to help myself. Then I wondered exactly how much of my foot I could shove into my mouth. "Don't answer that. I mean, of course you loved her. You asked her to marry you." And knowing he'd loved someone like that hurt so bad I couldn't do anything but ramble. Clearly.

"That's the funny thing. I honestly don't know. I've been thinking about it a lot lately, and... it's complicated. Our parents were close, she was sweet, and I always knew we'd end up together. I don't know if it was love so much as familiarity and acceptance. I don't think she loved me, though."

His obvious pain made my heart ache for him. "Why?" How could anyone *not* love Bull? He was so damn loveable it was all I could do to keep my hands off him.

He shrugged. "She didn't reach out to me. I thought we were thick as thieves, but when she was hurting and broken, she took her own life instead of coming to me. She didn't trust me. Fuck. I... I wish I would have done shit differently."

Unable to stay away from him any longer, I closed the distance between us and put my hand on his shoulder. "You were both so young. Just kids, trying to figure yourselves out. What do you honestly think you could have changed?

Head bowed, he answered, "I could have stayed home. I didn't have to join the Navy."

"You wanted to travel... to see the world. You think Amber would have wanted to keep you from that? Even if she did, you would have resented her for tying you down."

He stiffened. "I wouldn't have resented her."

"Not intentionally, but you would have. You love Seattle. You're a city boy at heart. I've never heard you say one positive thing about Shiner, Texas."

"We have decent beer."

I snorted. "Okay. One positive thing."

He frowned. "Well, I guess the joke's on me, because I still didn't get to see much of the world."

I rolled my eyes. I couldn't help myself. He was just so damn stubborn sometimes. "Listen, Bull-head, you're not dead. There's still plenty of time to see the world. I want to travel. I've never even been on an airplane, and I've always wanted to fly somewhere. Anywhere. Hawaii. Canada. Australia. Italy. I don't even care, I want to see them all. I'll come with you. We can save up money and travel around our work schedules."

His brow furrowed. "But didn't you hear what I told you? We can't be together, Lily."

Wait. What?

Was he brushing me off? Did he think that stroll down memory lane would shake me loose? Sure, it hurt to hear about his past, but it didn't change the way I felt about him one bit. "Um. Excuse me?" I asked. "Why the hell do you believe we can't be together."

"You look just like Amber. I'm talking spittin' image. It would be too much. I can't take you home. I mean, can you imagine what that would do to her parents? What it would do to mine? And you would hate it. Everyone looking at you sideways and talkin' shit...

Talk about resentment. How do you think you'll feel toward me when my family doesn't accept you?"

His eyes were pleading with me to understand, but I didn't. I didn't get what he was saying at all. Every excuse he coughed up was so far beyond my realm of understanding, it might as well have been Latin. "You don't think your family will accept me?" I asked. "Have you even told them about me?"

His mouth closed.

My heart sunk. "No. That's what I thought." My voice was trembling, and I couldn't stop it. Swallowing, I willed myself to be strong. I might never have another opportunity to spill my guts to Bull, and I refused to let my anger lay waste to this chance. "I never pegged you for a quitter."

He'd been playing with a hole in his jeans, but my response startled him out of it. His gaze snapped to mine, and whatever he saw in my expression caused him to shoot to his feet and run a hand over his head. "I'm not. You know I'm not."

"Yes, you are. You're quitting on us before you even give us a chance."

"God, Lily, be reasonable. You look like my dead fiancé. The daughter of my parents' best friends. I can't take you home. This thing between us can never be more than platonic."

Oh my God, he *was* giving up. I'd poked the bear, but I didn't really expect him to roll over. No, I wouldn't let him roll over. Not if I could help it. Not today. I stood and met his gaze once again. "How convenient for you."

"It's not convenient," he fired back, his face twisting in anger. "It's a shitty situation, but there's nothing I can do about it."

"For starters, you could have fucking talked to me before you made up your mind about how I'd feel. News flash, Bull, I've known about Amber for a few weeks now."

"You have?"

"Yes, but it hasn't changed the way I feel about you. I want to be with you. You're my best friend, but I want more than that. I want everything. I know shit between us won't be easy, but nothing in my life ever has been."

"I know!" He threw his hands up. "And you deserve more. Of all people, Lily, *you* should get easy. You deserve more than me."

He looked so broken, so absolutely devastated, I had to go to him. Desperate for his touch, I put my hands on his chest and met his gaze. A storm raged in his grey eyes, and the dark bags beneath them made me suspect he'd been having as much trouble sleeping over the past two weeks as I had. He looked like shit. Tortured, tormented, letting me go hadn't been any easier on him than it had been on me.

Well, it was time to put an end to this bullshit, because I wasn't going anywhere. Enough talking, it was time for Plan B.

I ripped my shirt over my head and tossed it to the floor.

Bull's eyes widened. His gaze shot to my chest, and the flames that ignited behind his eyes threatened to catch me on fire. "Wh-wh-what are you doing?" he asked.

I'd always been kind of shy about my body, but his obvious appreciation and the desperation that I was in danger of losing him emboldened me. I reached between my breasts to the front clasp of my lacy black bra. "Words are great and all, but I'm sick of talking." I released the clasp. My breasts sprang free, as I slid the straps over my arms and dropped it on the floor.

The cool air shocked my nipples, pebbling them immediately. Or maybe they stiffened in response to the bulge I could feel growing against my stomach. Either way, the girls needed some attention. Grabbing Bull's hands, I placed one on each breast. He squeezed, closing his eyes in agony.

"God, Lily, don't..."

"Don't what? We both want this."

"But we can't—"

"Hush. You've already told me the reason we shouldn't be together."

My voice came out husky and deeper than normal as the

callouses of his hands ran over my smooth skin. Electricity shot straight to my core, heating me from within. The room was chilly, but my body felt like it was on fire. I reached for the button of his jeans. He sucked in a breath as my fingers grazed the bare skin under his shirt. Unfastening the button, I tugged down his zipper.

"Now, let me show you all the reasons we should."

10

Bull

LILY WAS IN my space. I'd managed to avoid this very thing for more than two years, and suddenly, here we were. I should have never let her lead us into to my room. It was too private, too personal in here. Sure, there wasn't much to look at on the surface, but I had shit hidden away I wasn't ready to disclose yet. She'd already dragged my secrets out of me, leaving me feeling vulnerable and raw, and I wasn't ready to give up anything else quite yet.

I had every intention of trying to restore our friendship to what it was before.

I needed this girl.

Needed her random bizarre texts, and the annoying way she knew just when to drag me out of my own head and demand I take her out to eat or accompany her to the mall. What the fuck was wrong with me, that I even missed shopping with her? Shopping sucked ass, but somehow Lily managed to make everything fun. I needed her late-night phone calls that helped lull me to sleep when the demons of the past were holding sleep hostage. I craved her infectious laughter and its uncanny ability to make even the darkest days a little brighter.

I couldn't sacrifice our friendship for sex. I was standing firm, enforcing our boundaries and keeping a respectable distance between us.

And then, she took off her shirt and removed her bra.

Dressed, Lily was gorgeous. Topless, she was a fucking goddess, all smooth, milky skin and soft curves. She put my hands on her tits so I could feel the very definition of temptation. Hard nipples pressed against my hands, begging to be squeezed and licked. I tried like hell to resist, but her soft, cool touch against my stomach shattered any hope I had of self-control. I needed her friendship, but I also needed to taste her.

I needed to fuck her.

I was going to burn for this.

"Look at me," Lily said.

Her arousal leaked into her voice, making it huskier, sexier. Every word she muttered sounded like an invitation made directly to my cock. I didn't want to open my eyes. As long as they stayed closed, I could pretend this was just another dream. And dreams held no consequences. I could do all the things I'd ever wanted to do to her without fear of destroying our friendship. Ignoring her request, I slid my hands around her breasts, feeling their weight and enjoying the soft, smooth skin.

I could smell the hint of cinnamon on her breath from the two Fireball shots she'd taken. Mixed with the lingering vanilla berry body wash on her skin, the scent of her was some forbidden cocktail that made my mouth water. Everything about her invited me to touch, to lick, to claim. I wanted to watch my cock slide in and out of her mouth, to study the way she writhed under my tongue, to hear the sounds she made when I buried myself deep inside her.

Our very own porno played on the inside of my eyelids, as I imagined all the ways I'd wring pleasure out of her.

"Bull." She slid my cut down over my shoulders. The leather

rubbed against my skin, and I released her tits so the cut could fall down my arms. I felt lighter and less grounded without it, almost like I was floating.

"Look at me," she whispered.

I met her gaze. The golden flecks in her hazel eyes were practically glowing. Warm and inviting, like the welcome heat of a freshly stoked fire on a cold winter night. I wanted to step into her glow, to be surrounded by her warmth.

"We're friends," I said, trying to remind us both of what was at stake.

"I know. But I want more."

I suddenly realized I did, too. There was more than attraction pulling us together. If I let myself hope—let myself dream—I could see her in my bed. I could picture her wearing a white dress and walking down the aisle to meet me. What I couldn't imagine, was my life without her. What if we shot for the moon and came up short? I could end up stranded with no way to reach her, dying alone. "But what if we fuck it up? I can't lose you."

She cupped my face in her hands and looked into my eyes. Heavy, raw emotion stared back at me, and it was all I could do not to buckle under the weight of it. "You won't. I won't let you. You may be bull-headed, but we both know I'm more stubborn."

Could I trust her? Could I trust myself? Could we actually take this thing between us to the next level? There were so many hurdles in our way. "But my family…"

"I'm sure your family wants you to be happy." She slid her fingers up my abs, taking my T-shirt with her. "And if you'll stop overthinking everything and just allow yourself to enjoy this, I bet I can make you very happy."

Oh, I had no doubt she could. As if on autopilot, I raised my hands, letting her tug my shirt over my head. I couldn't resist her. I'd tried, and only lasted two, miserable, lonely weeks. I never wanted to go through that kind of hell again. She tossed the shirt aside and stared at me, biting her bottom lip as she gave my chest a full appraisal. The appreciation in her eyes made me feel good, but this was Lily, so I had to give her shit for it.

"Like what you see?" I asked.

"Shh. I'm tryin' to check out the goods. I've waited a long time for this. Don't distract me."

I opened my mouth to fire a snappy comeback, but the words died on my lips as the reality of the situation crashed into me.

We were doing this.

There was no holding back anymore.

Lily was mine, and I suddenly *had to* have her.

All the restraint I'd been honing for years broke free. She must have felt the change, because I lunged for her, and she met me in the middle. We mashed together in a tangle of arms and legs. Her lips landed on mine and I plunged my tongue into her mouth. Cinnamon and sin exploded on my tongue, making me want more. I pillaged her mouth, exploring every crevice like there'd be a test later, and I'd have to map it out.

She tugged at my jeans. She'd already unfastened them, and they easily fell to my ankles. Fumbling with her pants until I unfastened them, I broke the kiss long enough to slide them over her shapely hips and down her legs. They got hung up on her boots. She dropped down to take them off, and headbutted me in the gut.

Ouch.

"Ohmigod, I'm so sorry!" Lily said.

It hurt, but it could have been worse. She could have nailed me in the cock that was trying like hell to rip through my boxers and attack her. I'd probably have a bruise by my hip bone, but I couldn't find it in me to care. "It's okay. Nothing important was wounded."

Her gaze went to my boxers and her eyes widened. This time more carefully, she removed her boots, and tugged her pants over her feet. The denim got stuck on her heel, and she almost toppled over.

I caught her. "I don't remember you being this much of a klutz."

Lily's hazel eyes sparkled, laughing. I'd never met anyone who's eyes laughed like hers did. After all the shit she'd gone through, she still managed to find humor in life.

God, I loved her.

The realization made my chest squeeze so tight I must have winced, because concern flooded her eyes.

"What's wrong?" she asked.

"I..." Struggling to fit my emotions into words, I tried again, "I can't lose you... Angel." I'd never called her anything but Lily before, but the nickname just came out. And it fit. Lily had shown up at the darkest time in my life and helped me see the light. She was my fucking light. My angel.

Her expression softened, and then turned ravenous. Her lips mashed against mine so hard, a tooth nicked my lip. I tasted blood but didn't care. Our lips tangled, hands roamed, and we were back at it.

I needed more. I needed *all* of her.

With my tongue still down her throat, we hopped, scooted, and slid across the room.

We broke contact long enough for Lily to collapse on the bed. Lying there, in only a sexy black thong, with her hair fanned out around her, she even looked like an angel. A fallen angel, looking at my cock like she was about to attack it, far too perfect to be real. I wanted to fall to my knees and worship at her altar, paying homage to every soft, fleshy inch of her.

But I couldn't hold out that long.

My balls were already drawing up, pleading for me to get inside her. Precum leaked from my tip, making a mess out of the front of my boxers. I tried to kick off my boots, but the fuckers wouldn't budge. I didn't care. Shoving my boxers down around my ankles, I scooted to the nightstand and grabbed the box of condoms. They'd never been opened, and the plastic seal was a bitch. I scratched at it until I lost my mind and bit the damn thing.

Lily laughed.

"Oh, you think this is funny, do you?" I asked as my gaze once again swept over her form. God she was gorgeous. I could have gone my entire life just fantasizing about what she looked like under her clothes, but now that I'd seen her, I was done for. There was no way this would be a one and done event. There was no going back to the way things were before. I'd want to take her every way I could. The moment I slid inside her, I'd never be able to give her ass up.

But she deserves so much more...

"Stop thinking," Lily commanded. "You had your turn to make your case. Now it's my turn."

I finally extracted a condom from the box. She plucked it from my fingers, opened it, and slid it over my throbbing cock. All while staring at me like I was her favorite dessert.

Tavonte was right. She was like chocolate cake with my favorite filling. Forget wasting her, I couldn't even resist her. She was too rare and perfect.

God, her hands felt like silk as she stroked me through the condom.

I moaned, wanting her to stop so I didn't come and embarrass myself, but also wanting the relief she offered. She took me a little too close to the edge and I snapped out of my lust-induced craze to pull out of her grasp. I didn't want my first time with Lily to be in her goddamn hand.

"Lay back," I ordered. Her smile was wicked, and her eyes were lidded as she relaxed on the bed, once again putting her sexy body on display. I knew I couldn't hold out for much foreplay, but I wasn't a fucking animal, so I took my time to look her over, giving my cock a moment to calm down. Tracing a finger over her breast, I circled her nipple.

She sucked in a shuddering breath, and goosebumps formed across her flesh.

Amused, I let my finger continue its journey, sliding down to her narrow waist and over the swell of her hips. As I lightly brushed the insides of her thighs, she whimpered. It was the sexiest sound I'd ever heard, and I silently vowed to make it my mission in life to earn more of her sexy sounds. Lowering over her, I sucked one perfect nipple into my mouth.

"Oh, God," Lily rasped.

Loving her reaction, I circled her nipple with my tongue as I sucked. The nipple hardened in response. My hand between her thighs lightly brushed over her thong, teasing. She arched her back, trying to create more friction, but I pulled my hand away. Seeing her act all needy for me made my cock impossibly harder. It ached as I released her nipple and leaned back to get a good look.

Her thong was in my way.

Hooking my fingers in the sides, I slid it down over her hips. She arched her back to help my progress, and as I removed the garment, I slowly kissed my way down her legs.

By the time I finished, both sets of Lily's lips glistened with moisture. I'd tasted the set on her face, and suddenly needed to sample the other. I'd never gone down on a woman before, but I'd watched enough porn to know what to do.

I licked her seam.

I don't know what I'd been expecting her to taste like, but she was more. A hint of sweet. A hint of salt. Intriguing. Alluring. I needed more. She whimpered again. God, could her sounds be any sexier? I pushed back her lips and focused on the precious little bud of nerves they hid. The smell of her arousal wreaked havoc on my control, making me want to gobble her up.

Flattening my tongue, I licked her from entrance to clit, savoring the irresistible taste of her. Her body shuddered. I focused on the little bud of nerves again, sucking, licking, flicking. Everything I tried earned me a new reaction, a new sound, fisting sheets, arching back. I hadn't intended to bring her to release with my mouth, but the more she moaned and writhed, bucking her hips against my face, the more I realized I couldn't stop.

Her pleasure was everything.

I wanted her to come. Hell, I wanted to be the only man to bring her pleasure ever again. All her sexy little noises belonged to me. This wild, beautiful, incredible woman was mine, and I wanted her juices all over my face to prove it. Plunging a finger inside her channel, I ate her like she was my last meal.

Gasping, she grabbed my head with both hands and held me right where she wanted me. I licked and sucked, adding a second finger to the first. Curving the tips to hit what I hoped was her G-spot, I paid close attention to her reaction. Lips swollen, pussy pulsing, she bucked and writhed and fucked my face until she called out her release and collapsed. She was sated.

I'd fucking rocked her world.

Pride swelled in my chest as she trembled in aftershocks.

In the dim glow of my lamp, her entire body glistened, practically glowing. I sat up and withdrew my fingers. The scent of her was everywhere, driving me out of my fucking mind. I needed more of her taste, more of her. I popped my fingers into my mouth and cleaned them off. Eyes hooded, she watched me and waited. We'd shared so much over the years, and now we were sharing our bodies. There was something almost magical about the experience. I wanted it to last forever but didn't know how much longer I could hold out.

Rising up on my knees, I stroked myself, drawing her gaze to my cock. I thought about saying something witty or dirty, but it all sounded like bravado in my mind. Truth was, I was already reciting random work information in my head, trying to calm the fuck down enough that I wouldn't blow my load the second I slid inside her.

With the sweet, addictive taste of Lily still on my tongue, I released my cock and climbed on top of her. Our lips met again, and this time, our kisses were slower and more controlled. Full of emotion and promises. I didn't know what the fuck I could offer her, but whatever I had was hers. Every fucked up, lonely part of me, she could have it all. As our kisses deepened, she grabbed my cock and lined it up with her entrance, as desperate for me as I was for her. Hands on my ass, she pressed me against her.

Shit, she didn't have to tell me twice.

Sliding into her was the most incredible feeling I'd ever experienced. She was so damn hot and tight stars danced before my eyes. I felt... connected to her in a way I'd never been before. I couldn't get enough, but the pulsing of my cock promised I wouldn't last much longer. Gritting my teeth and trying my damnedest to think through the boring-ass steps of hooking up a tow were only going to get me so far.

I needed to make sure she enjoyed this as much as I did.

I squeezed a nipple between my fingers and started to rock in and out of her.

Three strokes.

That's all it took.

Three goddamn glorious, hide-my-head-in-shame strokes, and I came apart.

Embarrassed and shaky, I pulled out and apologized. "Sorry, Lil, I..."

Her eyes were warm and full of so much emotion I couldn't even concentrate on what I was about to say. On unsteady arms I settled myself beside her. Still disappointed in my performance, I started to roll over so I could go take care of the condom, but she grabbed my arm and stared at it. I was still shaking.

"Sorry," I repeated. "I don't know why I'm..." I'm what? Shaking like a goddamn leaf? Shit. What was wrong with me.

Her gaze met mine and understanding filled her eyes. "Is this... Were you a virgin, Bull?"

I wanted to deny it, but I'd apparently given myself away. "Why? Did I do something wrong?" She'd come, after all. Not on my cock, but on my tongue. That had to count for something. And if she stayed naked in my bed with that after-sex glow going on, I'd be ready for round two in no time.

"How?" She shook her head. "How the fuck did someone who looks like you make it into his mid-twenties still a virgin?"

"I've done lots of other shit," I said, sounding defensive even in my own ears. "We were raised in the church, Lil. Amber wanted to wait until we were married." As soon as the words came out of my mouth, I wanted to suck them back in. What kind of stupid motherfucker talks about his ex after sex? "I'm sorry," I blurted out. "I shouldn't have... No wonder you told me to stop talking."

Chuckling, Lily rubbed my arm. "It's okay." She kissed my cheek. My neck. The stubble tickled her, and she wrinkled her nose.

"Want me to shave that?" I asked.

"No!" she blurted out. Then she gave me a sheepish smile. "No. I like it. And I want to know everything about you. Everything. You don't have to watch what you say around me. Ever." Her lips met mine in a tender kiss.

"I love you," I whispered against her lips.

She froze.

I hadn't intended to tell her how I felt, but it was like I couldn't help myself. Hoping I hadn't scared her off, I pulled back enough to see her expression.

Eyes wide and brimming with emotion, she gaped at me. "I feel like I've waited my whole life to hear you say that."

A smile tugged at my lips. "So damn dramatic. You plannin' to tell me you love me, too?"

Squealing, she threw her arms around my neck and squeezed me to her. "I love you, I love you, I love you!" Releasing me, she dropped her gaze to my cock that was already well on the way to recovery. "Now go get rid of that condom, and I'll show you how much."

11

Lily

I COULDN'T BELIEVE I was in Bull's bed.

Two years of hoping, wishing, planning, and plotting had finally paid off, and it was everything I'd dreamed of and more.

He said he loved me.

He was scared of losing me.

As grandma would say, my cup was runnething over. Runnething? Was that even a word? I didn't care, because little aftershocks of pleasure had me feeling high as a fucking kite.

His tongue, oh my God!

I used to think Bull's sad, steel gray eyes were my favorite feature, but I bet he could lick the skin off a peach with that tongue. Hell, he'd licked the skin off my peach. I giggled, cracking myself up.

"What's so funny over there?" Bull asked.

I wanted to tell him, but held back. In the past, my dirty mind had always caused him to shut down. Our relationship had clearly changed, but he might still get uncomfortable and I wasn't ready to take that risk. "I'll tell you later."

Giving me a little side-eye, he tugged his boxers and jeans up his legs. We'd been so desperate to get it on, he hadn't even taken the time to remove his boots. That was kind of hot.

"You wanted me so bad you didn't even take off your boots," I said.

He tugged up the zipper, a splash of pink coloring his cheeks. "What can I say? You made one hell of a compelling argument."

But why was he getting dressed? We'd just declared our love for each other, and I'd made a promise to give him a physical demonstration of exactly how deep my feelings ran. I didn't want him dressed; I wanted his fine ass back in this bed.

"What's with the clothes?" I asked, unable to mask my uneasiness. Was he bailing on me? Did he regret what we'd done? Feeling exposed and vulnerable, I tugged up the sheet and covered my nakedness. I was trying not to panic, but if he told me to get dressed and leave, I had every intention of exploding in a mad rage of fury. I'd wreck the place. I'd go full-on Milton from *Office Space* and burn the place down. Okay, maybe not since I loved the Dead Presidents and would never do anything to leave the club homeless, but I'd do everything in my power to destroy Bull's bed. I'd worked my ass off to get into it, and if I couldn't enjoy it, nobody could.

"Gotta hit the restroom. I'll be right back." He slipped out of the door before I could respond.

I let out a breath, trying to exhale the crazy, borderline obsessive panic that kept threatening to choke me. Bull wasn't abandoning me. He just had to pee. There were a lot of emotions flying around, and he probably needed a moment to process. Obviously, I could use a few minutes to myself, too.

Standing, I went in search of my jeans. Not because I had any intention of dressing and leaving, but because I needed my phone to preoccupy me. I was disturbingly close to following him into the bathroom to make sure he didn't bail on me, and nobody wanted to see that level of crazy.

Our clothes were scattered all over the floor, so it took me a

Taming Bull

minute to retrieve my phone. Climbing back into Bull's bed, I narrowly resisted the urge to text everyone in my address book that I'd had mind-blowing sex, and the man of my dreams told me he loved me. I could barely keep the news in. Hell, I was tempted to climb up on the rooftop and scream out the details to all of Seattle.

But I was anxiously awaiting Bull's return and hoping he wasn't getting stuck so far in his own head I'd need to borrow his tow truck to drag him out.

My phone chimed with an incoming text.

Monica: Where are you? Carly said you and Bull are talking. Do you need backup? A rescue? Assistance with body disposal?

I belted out a laugh. Her willingness to commit a felony on my behalf hit me right in the feels. I had so much to tell her. Bull had just tickled my tonsils with his tongue—through my vagina—and now I was waiting for him to return from the bathroom so we could discuss the details of our upcoming nuptials. She should start working on her maid of honor speech. I drafted out my response, but realized it exceeded the limit of crazy I was allowed to let even Monica see, so I erased the text and tried again.

Me: No questions asked body disposal is probably the thing I love most about our friendship. Well, that and your homemade chocolate chip cookies. Thank you. I'm good, though. For now. I'll let you know if I snap and need a clean-up crew.

Monica's response consisted of a series of emojis. Knife, heart, casket, broom, party, Chinese food carton, and champagne glasses. Apparently, we'd stab him in the heart, bury him, sweep the whole thing under the rug, and then celebrate with Chinese takeout and champagne. If things didn't work out between me and Bull, it was a solid Plan B.

The door opened, and Bull stepped in. He closed the door, but his hand rested on the knob, like he hadn't decided to stay. He did not meet my gaze.

Fighting the urge to scream, I set my phone aside and gave him my undivided attention. "What's wrong?"

"Nothing." His tone was a little too defensive. "Now that we're done talking, I thought we might want to go back downstairs and catch the rest of the party."

Was he ashamed? He still wasn't looking at me. If he was second-guessing the best moment of my life, I was going to have to call Monica for that clean-up after all.

"No." I verbally put my foot down. "Clearly we're not done talking, because you're acting all standoffish again."

"I'm not standoffish, I'm... We still have a shit-load of obstacles to face, Lily."

"Lily? What the fuck happened to Angel? After two years, you've finally given me a nickname that doesn't suck. I like it. If you even think about revoking it, I'll buy some costume angel wings so I can use them to beat you upside your stubborn, foolish head."

Stubborn, foolish head lolling to the side, the look he gave me made it clear he thought I was being unreasonable.

"Don't look at me like that. You said you need me. Well, I need you, too. Yeah, we have shit to face, but we'll face it together. You're my best friend, Bull. I'm not letting you go. And, I'm not letting you overthink this so you can go back to acting like a little bitch."

"I'm looking out for you. That doesn't make me a little bitch. That makes me a concerned friend."

"No, a concerned friend would realize I don't need looking out for. I'm not after you for your family or your life in Shiner, Texas. I have a family." My hands flew up to encompass the entirety of the club. "I have a life. I have an education and a job. I even have a dog now."

His brow furrowed. "You do?"

"Yes. I'm happy and fulfilled. I don't need you to do that for me. I need you because I love you."

His shoulders relaxed and he let out a breath, finally meeting my gaze. "It won't be easy."

"Pfft. You don't want easy. She might look tempting, but easy's the village bicycle. She comes with burning STDs and raging regret."

He coughed to cover a surprised laugh, but not before it stole away a little more of the tension in his shoulders. Shaking his head, he admitted, "I never know what you're gonna say."

That made two of us. "Hey. Stick with me, kid, you'll never get bored."

The humor drained from his face. "Kid?"

I shrugged. "You did say you wanted it easy. It seems like a man would want more of a challenge."

That got a chuckle out of him. "What am I gonna do with you?"

"I have a few ideas. Let's see if you can guess." I gripped the top of the sheet that was curled up under my arms. "Am I gonna have to show you my boobs again as a clue?"

He considered me for a moment, his gaze drifting down over my body. The sheet didn't offer much coverage, and he could most likely see what his attention was doing to my nipples.

"Wouldn't hurt, but sex won't solve everything."

"Says who?" I scrunched up my nose. "You? By your own admission, you lack the experience necessary to make that judgement. That kind of conclusion can only come through... well, coming." Smirking, I let the sheet dip a little until it barely covered my nipples. "Lots and lots of coming."

Grinning, he valiantly tried to keep eye contact despite his apparent desire to leer at my exposed flesh. I could almost see his eyeballs bouncing south. "Fair enough."

It felt so right to banter with him like this. Comfortable. Bull felt it, too. He'd taken a few steps closer, the remaining tension had drained from his body, and his eyes were filled with amusement. I'd just needed to remind him how good we were together. This would work. I didn't need him to save me from his past; I was my own knight. Patting the bed beside me, I said, "Ass. Here. Now."

"Are you always this bossy after sex?" he asked. But he also started walking.

Patting myself on the back, I decided to give his ego a well-deserved boost. "I think it was the orgasm. I've never come that hard in my life."

He straightened. "You liked that?"

"Liked it?" I scoffed. "If I had known your tongue was that talented, I would have sat on your face years ago. I think I turned Pentecostal there for a minute."

I didn't even know where this shit was coming from, but the way his eyes lit up were worth every degree of heat that flooded my cheeks.

Beaming with pride, Bull wandered over and sat on the bed. I released my hold on the sheet and let it slide down my body before climbing around to kneel at his feet. This time, his damn boots were coming off. Trying to project a calm self-confidence I didn't feel while I was naked as the day I was born and he still had his jeans on, I untied one boot.

"I can do that," Bull said. If the hoarseness of his voice didn't give him away, the bulge in his jeans sure would have. He was enjoying the show. Good.

Pushing his hand away, I replied, "I want to."

Removing one boot, then the other, I took off his socks and stood, putting my breasts right in Bull's face. He swallowed and forced his gaze to rise to my face. Trying not to smirk, I held out my hand. He accepted, and I hefted him to his feet. Well, I tugged, and he got the drift and stood.

Unfastening his pants, I pushed both jeans and his boxers down his legs. He stepped out, and I kicked them aside and dropped back down to my knees. I took his massive, hard cock in my hand and smiled up at him. The heat in his eyes threatened to consume me. His Adam's apple bobbed up and down as he gulped.

A drop of pre-cum coated the head of his dick. I licked it clean.

He swore.

More precum leaked out. I fought back a smile and ran the head over my mouth like I was painting my lips with his flavor. Pulling back, I held his gaze and licked my lips.

He let out a strangled sound.

Encouraged by his reaction, I slid his cock past my now moistened lips. Taking him in slowly, I explored every inch of his shaft with my tongue. Touching, tasting, probing. The velvety hard texture of him against my tongue was strangely erotic. Every lick and suck I enjoyed sent a wave of heat straight to my core. Moisture collected between my thighs, and I squeezed them together. The friction felt so damn good. Bull moaned, and the sound went straight to my pussy. I had no idea sucking dick could be such a huge turn-on.

His jaw ticked and his fists clenched as he struggled to maintain control. Needing more relief of my own, I dropped one hand to my slit and massaged until I couldn't remember which one of us I was trying to get off.

"Fuck. You are so goddamn sexy," Bull said, his hands going to my head. "My angel."

His voice trembled when he said it, making my heart swell. Swirling my tongue, I ran it up and down his shaft. He moaned again. Sealing my mouth around his cock, I did my best to suck out his fucking soul. It was mine now, and I needed his ass to remember that. His body quivered, and another wave of heat went straight to my core.

We were both teetering on the edge of release when he stopped me. I wanted to finish, but he slid his hips out of my grasp and pulled me up his body. I stood before him, breathing heavily and wondering how to get his cock back in my mouth.

Bull's eyes were wild, crazy. Grabbing my face in both his hands, he kissed me. I wanted him to devour my mouth, but he kept the kiss sweet and tender. I had the feeling he was trying to give us both a moment to calm down.

"Did you not like that?" I asked as he broke off the kiss.

"Like? Fuck, I loved it," he breathed. "Stopping you was probably the hardest thing I've ever done."

I smirked. "Pun intended."

He smirked back. "Indeed. I don't want to come in your mouth yet. After my last performance, I... I want another shot."

Oh. That made sense. Well, if he needed to redeem his manly pride, who was I to stop him? I brushed my lips against his.

He deepened the kiss, and his warm hands drifted down my neck to my shoulders leaving a heated trail in their wake. Gently skimming my arms, his soft touch gave me goosebumps before landing on my breasts. He pinched and teased my nipples, cupped my breasts, and met each of my needy whimpers with a groan of his own. Yes, he was torturing me, but he was torturing himself, too. The knowledge that we were suffering together was comforting. His hands continued their exploration over my hips. They cupped my ass and pulled me against him until I couldn't tell where he ended, and I began. His hard cock pressed into my stomach, making me want it even more. One hand went up to my back to hold me in place, while the other went down to play with my pussy.

I was on fire. My body was a goddamn inferno. I needed him to either throw a log on the fire or extinguish it.

Pulling away from his lips, I whispered, "Please?"

Knowing what I needed, he reached for the nightstand, but I grabbed his hand, stopping him.

"I'm on the pill. We don't need those." He loved me, and I loved him. Armed with the knowledge I was Bull's first, I had every intention of being his last. I didn't want anything between us ever again.

Abandoning the box of condoms, his hand wrapped back around me and he lowered us both to the bed. This time, when he slid inside of me, I was the one who about lost control.

"Fuck. It feels even better bare," he breathed, gritting his teeth. "I didn't think it was possible, but holy shit."

Okay, so maybe we were both riding the edge. He managed to get himself under control, though, and in no time, he was giving me exactly the friction I needed right in the place I needed it most. Unable to hold on anymore, I threw back my head and called out his name as I came.

I was in Bull's bed.

He loved me, and I loved him.

If he ever so much as thought about shaking me loose again, I'd just have to fuck him into submission.

Piece of cake.

12

Bull

LILY REALLY DID have a dog. She told me she did, and it's not that I didn't believe her, but her living situation didn't exactly lend itself to pets. It was by the grace of God—and the women of Ladies First—she had a place to stay at all, so I had a hard time imagining her bringing a dog into the situation. When she used him as a reason not to stay over, I thought she was brushing me off. I mean, a dog? Talk about a lame excuse. Especially after we'd made so much headway.

I couldn't understand why she'd worked so hard to get into my bed and didn't want to stay. Sure, the first time we'd fucked had been embarrassingly quick, but I'd made sure she was taken care of before I came. And then there'd been other orgasms... both hers and mine. Yeah, it was my first time, but she was walking a little funny, so I knew I'd given it to her pretty good. Regardless, her asking me to bring her home had still done a number on my pride.

Parking my bike, I helped her off before dismounting and walking her to the door. She didn't want to stay with me, so I intended to kiss her goodnight and be on my way, but Lily tugged me through the front door before I could retreat.

"At least come in and meet him," she said.

"Is he stuffed?" I asked, swearing under my breath. If she was ditching me for some plush dog, I was going to lose my shit.

"What?" She giggled. "No. Look. There he is."

Stretched out over a dog bed in the living room, the pit bull mix eyed us, but didn't otherwise move.

"You sure he's not stuffed?" I asked, keeping my voice low. It was well past midnight, and Monica had texted Lily to let her know they were leaving the party over an hour ago. They were probably fast asleep by now, and I wanted to keep it that way. The entire club would know that Lily and I had taken our relationship to the next level soon, but I was enjoying our privacy for now. I didn't want to wake anyone up and have them speculating about why we smelled like sex and couldn't stop touching each other.

She elbowed me. "He's had a long day and he's tired." Lily crouched down, slapping her hands against her thighs, "Come on, boy."

His tail wagged. Twice.

This was the dog she'd been so excited to get home to? "I've never seen such a lethargic mutt in my life."

She shot me a glare. "He's not lethargic. He's conserving energy so he can pounce on your rude ass. Get up, Brahma. Come meet Bull."

"Brahma?" I asked. Being from Texas, I was all too familiar with the breed of bull, and couldn't help but make the connection to my road name. "Did you name him after me?"

"Absolutely not." She did her best to sound offended, but couldn't quite hide her smile. "I was mad at you. If I attached your name to something, I'd want to kick it, and I'd never abuse a dog. I might have turned a picture of you into a dart board in my room, though."

I chuckled. "I probably deserved that."

The dog finally rose and waddled over to Lily.

"Look at his coloring. He looks like a Brahma. He's tough and scary like one, too. Aren't you my big, terrifying protector?" She scratched under his chin and his tongue about hit the floor.

When Lily stood, he wandered over to me, sniffed my hand, and then plopped himself down at my feet to roll over and show me his belly.

"Big, terrifying protector, my ass." I said.

Lily scooted closer to me, brushing my arm with her fingertips. It's like she didn't want to stop touching me, and I understood the feeling all too well. I brushed against her.

"Brahma has this great sneak attack. He pretends to be all sweet and loving, but when you bend down to scratch him, he goes for you jugular. He's trying to get you down to his level. It's a ploy."

"Uh-huh." I caught her hand in mine and bent to scratch Brahma's belly with my free hand. His eyes rolled back in his head and one leg thumped against the floor. "That's basically the opposite of attacking me."

"Yeah, of course he's not gonna attack you right now. He knows you're not dangerous," she said. "He doesn't attack guests. He's super smart. But if you snuck into the house and I wasn't with you... you'd be leaving on a stretcher. Come on. I'll get some ice cream." She towed me toward the kitchen.

"Why are you making up this shit?" I asked.

She shrugged. "I'm not. I can tell when a guy's protective. You are, and so is he."

Rather than following us to make sure Lily was okay in my presence, Brahma had gone back to his dog bed. I wanted to question Lily's intuition, but since she'd lumped me in there with him, I couldn't. I didn't know about the dog, but I'd do anything I could for her. She wasn't wrong about that.

After we'd gone a few rounds in the sack, Lily and I had spent hours talking in my bed, trying to catch up on the past two weeks. Well, she talked while I listened and answered questions. It was crazy how quickly we fell back into our friendship, but this time, shit was different. As she told me about her days, I couldn't help but hate all the time I'd missed out on. I should have been here, helping her study for her tests. I should have been the one to buy her a celebratory drink after she'd passed. She was my best friend, and I'd let her down. At the time, I thought my intentions were good, but with the benefit of hindsight, I saw exactly how wrong I'd been. Silently vowing to make it up to her, I listened for hours, doing my best to hear everything she said and what she didn't.

Lily needed me. And I was damn well going to be there for her from here on out.

I also spent those hours learning all I could about her body. She had a mole behind her left ear. I'd never noticed it before, but now that I had, it became one of my favorite places to kiss. I loved the way her breath would catch every time my lips grazed the sensitive skin.

I could kiss every inch of her body, except her neck. She was irrationally ticklish there, unable to handle the contact of my whiskers against her soft skin regardless of what we were doing. I could be buried deep inside her, about to make her come, and one kiss on her neck would drive her into a fit of giggles and make her try to squirm out from under me.

She loved it when my fingers trailed up and down her back. Not like a massage, just a light touch, barely skimming the skin as I played dot-to-dot with her freckles.

It's probably a good thing she had me bring her home, because neither of us would have gotten a lick of sleep if she'd stayed over. Her body was just too damn tempting, holding too many secrets I still wanted to explore. Now that I'd had her, it was like I couldn't get enough.

Lily grabbed a gallon of ice cream from the freezer, then released my hand to retrieve bowls from the cupboard. I couldn't tell you if she moved, or I did, but our lower bodies stayed connected. We'd have to separate eventually, but I wasn't ready to.

Not yet. I kept my hand on her lower back as she scooped dessert and led me to the table. As we sat, our legs intertwined.

Touching Lily just seemed right.

"How did the podium turn out?" Lily asked.

She'd helped me sand and stain the old beat-up gift Wasp bought for Link, but she hadn't gotten the chance to see the finished product. Excited to show off my work, I tugged out my phone and pulled up the pictures. As she swiped through them, she grinned.

"I can't believe this is the same podium. I love the metal strips you added. Awesome touch. Looks a little steampunk." She handed me back my phone. "Make me something?"

"Like what?"

"I don't know. Something special."

"I didn't make the podium."

She rolled her eyes. "Okay. Buy me some old piece of furniture and refinish it. Better?"

I tried to think of something to get her, but I was having trouble focusing. She had a drop of ice cream on her bottom lip and it was terribly distracting. I couldn't help but wonder what the dessert would taste like from her lips. Closing the distance between us, my tongue snaked out and sampled her lips.

Lily's eyes dilated. Her gaze darted to my mouth.

It was all the invitation I needed. Ice cream forgotten, I cradled her face in my hands and crushed my lips against hers. We'd fucked multiple times, but it wasn't enough. I needed more. Her hands landed on my head, mussing my hair as she held me to her. My body reacted instantly, ready to plunge back into that tight, welcoming pussy. I should be exhausted, but I couldn't get enough of her. Sex had turned me into some insatiable beast, and all I wanted was Lily. I was seriously considering carrying her fine ass upstairs and seeing how many more orgasms I could wring from her when she pulled away and brandished her spoon like a sword, keeping me at bay.

"No. Stop. And don't look at me like that." Cheeks pink, lips swollen, eyes wild, she looked like she wanted to jump on my lap, but she kept that damn spoon between us.

"Look at you like what?" I put my hand on her inner thigh and she all but melted against me. "Like I want more of what we had earlier?"

"Yes." She snatched my wandering hand and put it on the table. "It's against the rules to take visitors upstairs and trust me, you do *not* want to make Monica angry. She hulks out. Turns green, rips her clothes, everything. It's not a pretty sight. In fact, you should get back to the fire station before we do something crazy like try to get around her rules by doing the nasty right here on this table."

I liked that idea. A lot. Judging by the way my cock throbbed against my zipper, it was all-in, as well. "It wouldn't be upstairs, so technically, we'd be in the clear."

"See, that logic right there is what's going to get us killed. I can't go back to being homeless. I have a dog to think about, and you saw how much he loves his bed." Standing, Lily took her ice cream and made a hasty retreat into the kitchen, putting a shit-ton of unwelcome space between us. Leaning against the island, she took a bite while watching me.

What I wouldn't have done to be her ice cream...

She was right, though. I had no desire to offend Stocks or Monica by stomping on their hospitality, so I kept my distance as we finished our treat. Then, I gave her a kiss goodbye and forced myself to leave before I did something that could get us both in trouble. I'd gotten three steps away from the house when she ran out after me. I stopped, and she grabbed my face and directed my gaze onto hers.

"I love you, Bull. Promise me you won't go home and start overthinking everything. I want this—I want you and everything that comes with you—and I will fight for you if I need to. You're not getting rid of me, so don't even think about trying."

I didn't think I could force myself to shake Lily if I wanted to. I was having enough trouble just walking away from her for the night. I dropped my forehead to hers and breathed in her clean, sweet scent, letting it ground me. "I love you, too. I'll try."

Back in the day when I'd first prospected with the club, our parties didn't end before sunrise. We'd close the place down, stumble upstairs, and sleep the day away. But now that half the club was married with kids, all-nighters were a thing of the past. By the time I got back to the fire station, it was almost 2:00 a.m., and the party was winding down. All the married couples and kids had cleared out hours ago. Zombie and Frog were on one pool table, and the other was empty. Morse was sitting in a corner with his laptop, and Tavonte was alone at the bar, nursing another beer.

Since he had an early flight, I was surprised to see him still up. I poured myself a large glass of water and sat beside him.

"Saw you leave with Lily," Tavonte said, playing with the bottle. "Everything okay between you two now?"

"Yeah." Unable to help myself, I smiled. Just thinking about my angel had me grinning like a goddamn guilty devil. "We're good."

Tavonte eyed me and smiled. "Glad to hear it. You talked everything out?"

"Yeah. Thanks for the push. I needed that. I'm still worried about my family and don't know what the fuck's gonna happen when I show up on their doorstep with Lily on my arm, but we're committed to trying this." Mom would probably pass out and Dad would freak out and ask if I'd lost my damn mind. And Lily? Well, she'd take it all in stride. She'd probably win them over with her uncanny ability to wriggle into people's hearts.

Tavonte chuckled. "A word of advice… warn them first."

"Yeah. It's probably past time for me to have a conversation with the folks."

"It's amazing the shit you can fix by opening up and actually talking to people," he deadpanned.

"Smartass." I tried to glare at him, but doubted it worked since I couldn't seem to stop grinning. "Don't you have a flight in the morning? Shouldn't you be asleep?"

"Yeah." He shrugged. "I should be, but... I'm worried about what I'll be walking into at home. I've tried to call Kiana a few times, but she's not answering. Mom told me all she knows, which isn't much. My sister started hanging out with some hood rat. Mom told her to stay away from him and focus on her schoolwork, but my sister can be stubborn as hell. Mom caught her sneaking back through her bedroom window the other morning. Doesn't know where she was and how long she was gone. Mom demanded answers, but Kiana lost her mind, talkin' about how she's in love and shit."

"Maybe she is?" I suggested.

He leveled a hard look at me. "No man worthy of my sister is gonna want her crawling through windows and sneaking around like some side-piece. The shit-for-brains isn't even in high school. He's a grown ass man and has no business fuckin' with a sixteen-year-old girl. Mom's worried Kiana is gonna get knocked up. Or worse."

"Shit. Sorry. I didn't realize he was older. Thought it was just a couple of teenagers being crazy. This guy sounds like a real bastard. You need any help, be sure to let me know. I can fly out and help you bust some heads."

"Thanks, brother. I can take care of my own, but I appreciate the offer."

"If you change your mind and need me, I'm there. Besides, the travel might be nice." My talk with Lily had reminded me of that dream. There were still so many places I wanted to see—shit I wanted to do—and it was nice to know I wouldn't have to travel alone. "I've always wanted to see Nashville. Bet Lily would like that, too."

Tavonte nodded. "My mom's one hell of a cook. I'm tellin' you, it'd be worth the trip for her homemade mac-n-cheese and biscuits and gravy. Mhm-mhm. Okay. Just thinkin' about Mom's cookin' has me feelin' a lot better about headin' home. Sure, I may have to kill a motherfucker, but at least I'll get some good meals out of it. Once I'm settled and have this shithead dealt with, you and Lily can fly out and visit. I'll take you around to all the hot spots."

"Deal." I drained my water and stood. "I gotta get to bed. Gotta work tomorrow and I'm already gonna be hating life. I'll see you in the morning before you head out, right?"

Tavonte nodded. He stood and we clasped hands, patting backs, before heading in our separate directions.

My phone buzzed with an incoming text, so I tugged it out of my pocket.

Lily: Have you ever wondered why local bars can only sell alcohol until 2:00 am?

The question was so classic Lily, I laughed out loud as I headed for my room.

Me: Can't say I have.

Lily: Well, I Googled it, and can't find a reason. I did find a pretty color-coded time chart, though. Apparently it's illegal for bars in Washington to serve between the hours of 2 and 6 am. Why? Does the ghost of inebriation drunk dial people and magically turn them into alcoholics at 2:01? I need to know.

Me: The bigger question here is what bars are open at 6 am, and why have we never gone to one?

Lily: See? Every time you feed my insatiable curiosity like that, my panties melt a little.

Taming Bull

I groaned at the visual that accompanied her text wishing she was waiting in my bed, rather than across town in her own.

Me: Don't make me turn this car around and ravage you again.

Lily: I miss you already.

Me: Same. Go to sleep, Angel.

Lily's response was made up of a series of emojis: happy face, heart, smiley face with a halo, bed, dog, happy face, and heart. I went to bed smiling for the first time in a long ass time.

13

Lily

I WAS ON top of the world.

Not literally, thank God, because heights and I had never gotten along. But metaphorically speaking, I couldn't get any higher if I was making special brownies with Snoop Dogg and Martha Stewart.

I was also exhausted.

Cherished memories of the moments I'd spent in Bull's bed kept me awake long after he replied to my last text. Unlike Bull, I was no virgin, but sex had never felt wrapped in feelings like this before. Emotions bubbled inside of me, making it impossible to sleep. I spent most of the night reveling in the afterglow of our declarations of love, still unable to believe he'd finally given in to his desire for me.

Despite all odds, I'd busted out of the dreaded friend zone.

Take that, you motherfuckin' black hole!

And I didn't even have to become a subatomic particle to do so. Good thing, since I liked science about as much as I liked heights and didn't even know what a subatomic particle was. According to

Google, it was the only way to escape a black hole, but I'd proven all internet search engines wrong.

I wanted to celebrate. There should be balloons and some girl-power song blasting in the background while I sipped champagne. I'd never had champagne, but I was certain this occasion called for some bubbly. Instead of partying it up in honor of my achievement, everyone was asleep, and I needed to keep my excitement bottled and stare at the backs of my eyelids until my mind went into hibernation mode. I had a full day scheduled and I needed sleep.

By the time my alarm went off at 7:00 a.m., I'd gotten maybe three hours of shut eye and wanted nothing more than to turn off the annoying buzz and go back to dreamland. But there was no rest for over-committers. I'd volunteered to help Julia with Marcus on my last day off before my apprenticeship started, and I wasn't about to let the Wilsons down.

Julia's bookstore wasn't far from the fire station, about six blocks from the shelter. Too close to justify the use of my dwindling funds to purchase a bus ticket, so I decided to get some fresh air and exercise and jog the distance. Once upon a time, I used to run track, and I was still in relatively good shape. Or so I thought. By the time I arrived at the bookstore, I was gasping for air like a two-pack-a-day smoker who needed caffeine and a good stretch, stat.

Since Julia was still nursing the baby, I was terrified there'd be no coffee. I should have known better. Like any proud Seattleite, she not only had coffee, she had the good stuff: so dark and flavorful it should be illegal. The pot had just finished brewing when I walked into the shop, and between the smell of old books and freshly brewed coffee, I was in fragrance heaven.

I headed into the kitchenette and looked over the collection of coffee cups. Several had funny sayings or cute kitten pictures, but since I planned to cart Marcus around, I needed a safer vehicle for my addiction. Finding a lidded tumbler, I added enough flavored creamer to preserve my body until the end of time and went in search of my charge.

"I see why you're so reluctant to give this place up," I said, my gesture encompassing the space.

Julia didn't have to work. She had a trust fund and an inheritance from her deceased ex-asshole who'd foolishly neglected to scrub her from his will. But the bookstore was her first love, and she refused to let it go. And, since Havoc was the type of man who'd move heaven and earth for his wife, they'd found a way to make it work. Spade and Stocks had helped him move out the counter to put in a temporary wall that created a small nursery area. With a swing, playpen, and bassinet, Marcus was all set. I doubted Julia even needed my help, but since her one employee needed to start taking Sundays off, Havoc didn't want Julia and Marcus at the bookstore alone.

"I love it here. It was my sanctuary for years, and without it, I never would have met Havoc." Julia smiled fondly. "Besides, Tap has been helping me with social media marketing, and business has been picking up. The work is easy—perfect for a new mom—and I set my own hours."

I chuckled, recognizing her spiel for what it was. "Nice speech, but you don't have to convince me." I inhaled deeply. "The combination of books and coffee alone sold me."

Marcus had started fussing in his bassinet, so I slid him into his baby sling and affixed it to my body, freeing up my hands so I could drink coffee and help Julia.

When she realized what I was doing, her gaze fell on my lidded tumbler. "Thank you for thinking of that."

I saluted her with my drink. "Not my first rodeo. Gotta keep our little man safe and burn-free."

Nodding, she studied a book's spine before sliding it into its spot on the shelf. "Do you like to read, Lily?"

"Yes."

If she was surprised, she didn't show it. "What sort of books do you prefer?"

"Fantasy, YA, new adult, romance."

She added another book to the shelf. "Was there a particular person or event that turned you into a reader?"

"When I was little, my grade school used to host reading challenges. I was pretty competitive, so I borrowed one of the approved books from the library and got in on the challenge. My parents had just split up, leaving me with my grandma, and I was... struggling with reality. Books became my escape from the bullshit."

She nodded. "I get that. When my first marriage started falling apart, it was easier to lose myself in the love stories of others than it was to deal with the fact my ex was a manipulative, cheating douche canoe who wouldn't know love if someone rammed it into his mangina."

"Mangina?" I asked, unfamiliar with the term.

Julia shrugged. "What can I say? Some men are just pussies."

I belted out a laugh. No wonder Havoc had fallen for Julia. She knew the best words and had an amazing sense of humor. We went to work and between the constant caffeine, the delicious gyros and sugary baklava Julia had delivered for lunch, Marcus's sweet snuggles, and Julia's ridiculous stories about her crazy-ass family, I made it through the day. By the time Havoc arrived to relieve me, I was so far beyond exhausted I could barely feel my feet, but my cheeks hurt from smiling so much.

It had been my pleasure to help Julia and I didn't expect compensation, but when Havoc slapped a fifty into my hand, his hard-ass look didn't leave any room for argument. "You gave me peace of mind so I could work," he said. "Trust me, that's worth more than this fifty. You need a ride home?"

His arms were full of baby. He had bags under his eyes and looked like his first day back to work had taken five years off his life. He needed to be here with his wife and son.

"Nah. Thanks, but I got it."

He was far too stoic to sigh in relief, but I could tell he wanted to. "Next Sunday?" he asked.

"Of course. I had a blast." I kissed Marcus's forehead, gave Julia a hug goodbye, and took off.

Body feeling like Jell-O, with fifty unexpected dollars in my pocket and the threat of being late hanging over my head, I opted out of jogging and hopped a bus home. My bed called to me with promises of soft, comfy sleep, but I didn't have time to answer. I'd made a promise of my own. Leashing Brahma, I led him the few blocks to the park. By the time we arrived, I was regretting every single commitment on my time I'd ever made, but the way Johnny's face lit up when he saw Brahma made my sore feet and tired legs worth every overbooked, worn-out minute of my life. Physically, I was running on fumes, but emotionally, my tank couldn't have been fuller. Especially when Shelly wiped away a tear and thanked me again for meeting up with them.

The park bench called to me, and I stretched out across it, my eyelids so heavy I could barely keep them open. Shelly looked at me like I'd lost my mind, and I didn't have the heart to tell her that sleeping on park benches was nothing new for me. That kind of talk made people uncomfortable, but when I was homeless, I'd learned to sleep where I could.

There was no shame in grabbing a few winks on a bench.

To make her more at ease, I stood to keep myself from nodding off.

Johnny and Brahma played ball for a little over an hour, until my dog was almost as tuckered out as I was. The last time Johnny threw him the ball, Brahma glanced at it, and collapsed in the grass, refusing to fetch. I'd never felt so spiritually connected to an animal in my life. I held up my fist in solidarity and imagined him doing the same. Shelly and Johnny took off, and I coaxed Brahma to his feet with promises of treats and a nap. The walk from the park to the shelter took forever. When we finally dragged our asses over the threshold, Brahma went straight for his water bowl, and I collapsed face down on the floor of the living room, hoping I'd never have to move again.

No such luck. Moments later, footsteps preceded the feel of something soft hitting my back. It rolled down my side, across the floor, and under the couch. Plastic poop bags. Great.

"He shit in the back yard while you were with Julia. It's to the left of the porch," Monica told me.

Of course he did. I glared at the guilty pooper—who was curled up on his doggie bed—but he looked away. It took everything in me to push myself up off the floor and retrieve the poop bags, but I did it.

"And don't think you're getting out of telling me what happened between you and Bull last night," Monica added as I headed for the back door.

By the time I cleaned up Brahma's mess and fed him, Bull was off work. He called me, sounding every bit as exhausted as I felt. Since I had to be up early in the morning to start my apprenticeship, we both decided to call it a night early. I missed him, but I needed sleep. I ate, dodged Monica's questions about my relationship with Bull, and then took Brahma out again before we went upstairs and passed out.

"I've never been in an adult relationship before. It's weird," I told Monica. We were sitting at the kitchen table, it was Wednesday, and the first few days of my apprenticeship had passed in a blur of introductions, paperwork, and policies and procedures manuals. It felt a lot like being back in school. The newness was wearing off, and my time and attention were focusing back on Bull. I hadn't seen him since Saturday night—well, early Sunday morning—and I missed him. A lot. Between my early mornings and his swingshifts, our work schedule was out of whack, and we hadn't been able to connect in person. We texted and talked on the phone every day, but it wasn't the same.

Monica arched an eyebrow at me. "Never? When was your last relationship?"

"High school. It was so different. We saw each other every day at school and hung out on the weekends, no real responsibilities keeping us apart. You know?"

"Ah. High school. To be honest, I don't even remember it."

I didn't buy that for a minute. "You're not that old."

"Oh, I know. But I took a lot of advanced classes and volunteered at a hangar. I was busy workin' on my future and didn't really buy in to the high school experience."

I did. High school was fun for me. Classes, dances, spirit week, football and basketball games, I'd enjoyed being part of it all. I didn't have much, but I had Grandma. We had a warm, safe home, and the cupboards were never bare. Looking back, I realized I'd taken that all for granted until Grandma passed away. Shortly after, the bank foreclosed on the house and reality smacked me right upside the head.

Barely eighteen, fresh out of high school, mourning Grandma's death, with less than a thousand dollars to my name saved up from babysitting and my after-school waitressing job, I didn't have many options. I could have probably stayed and rented a room from a friend's parents, but my dad's greedy ass had come sniffing around for a life insurance policy, certain he was entitled to more, but Grandma didn't have anything to leave behind. He'd taken everything she had already.

With Grandma gone, there was nothing left for me in Georgia. Needing to get out of there, I hopped a bus and rode it until the end of the line. Seattle was home now.

Over the years, Monica had dragged all that information out of me, but apparently, we'd never talked about my past relationships. "The last guy I dated—Luke—was a world-class douche bag. But he was hot. Wavy, blond hair that he kept a little long and shaggy, and beautiful blue eyes. He was only about five-foot-ten, but he was a wrestler. Worked out a lot and had a nice body. His dad owned the Ford dealership, and they lived in a big house on the good side of the railroad tracks. When he took an interest in little ol' me, I was so excited I about lost my mind. Didn't take much for him to convince me to sneak off campus with him. I lost my virginity in the backseat of his Mustang."

"Lily!" Monica gasped, sounding positively scandalized.

"What?"

"The back seat of a car? Seriously? That's so cliché."

"It's not like it was some beater. Metallic blue, five-point-oh engine, leather seats, my clothes practically melted off."

She chuckled. "I can't believe you."

"Yeah? Well, Luke was smooth. Knew what he was doin.' He took me to this secluded spot beside the Chattahoochee. It was beautiful and I felt special and treasured. He could have had any girl in that school, and he chose me."

"To fuck him in a car. Yay, you. Lil, that's not how treasure should be treated."

"Why so judgy?" I asked. "Haven't you ever gone mad with lust and ripped someone's clothes off in the back seat before?"

Monica leveled a look at me. "Queens do not fuck in vehicles."

"At all?" Surely some cars had to be acceptable. "What about a Lambo or something equally as expensive and flashy?"

Her forehead wrinkled as she thought about it for a second. "Too cramped. I gotta stretch out and get my cardio on. It's all about multi-tasking. If I can get a few orgasms *and* a good workout... shit. I'm all about that."

I laughed. "Okay, something bigger? Maybe a Hummer?"

"Tempting, but no. Okay, I'd be willing to get freaky in one of those decked out tour busses. Or a luxury camp trailer if Stocks ever manages to drag me camping."

"I'm pretty sure that's called glamping. Glamor camping. It's not real camping."

"It's the only camping you'll ever see me do." She shrugged. "Regardless, sex in a Mustang is out."

"Well, it only happened once," I defended. "The school called Grandma and told her I ditched my afternoon classes, and she was waiting for us when Luke dropped me off. She made such a scene, he never so much as looked at me again. God, I was angry with her. Thought she ruined my senior year and my one chance at true love. But it turned out Luke wasn't the amazing catch I thought he was. While we were supposedly dating, the bastard knocked up one of the cheerleaders. I bet he even took her to our spot to do it. Come to think of it, I probably should have taken a black light to the backseat of his 'stang. Bet it could have told me all I needed to know about the womanizing asshole."

"Please tell me you ripped off his balls and fed them to him."

I chuckled. "Nope. I left that privilege to the parents of the cheerleader. They took Luke to court and nailed him with child support. Eighteen years of garnished wages should teach him for being a cheating piece of shit."

"And they say there's no justice in the world." Monica rubbed her forehead. "I do feel bad for the girl, and the child, though. Nobody should have to be conceived by a couple of high schoolers in the back seat of a car. You were lucky to get out of that mess. Your grandma sounds like a solid judge of character."

My fingers instinctively went to the necklace hiding under my T-shirt. "She was. I wish she was here now. She'd love Bull."

Monica smiled. "I bet she would. How are things between the two of you?"

I knew kissing and telling broke some cardinal rule of relationships, but there was no keeping anything from Monica. I'd held out until Tuesday after work, but she'd eventually broken down my walls and made me spill my guts. "We're still texting and calling, but I miss him. It's hard working different shifts and days. I wish we didn't have all these stupid adult responsibilities so we could go find a peaceful spot beside a river and—"

"You are *not* to fuck in a car again."

"He doesn't even own a car, and I really doubt we could do it on his bike. That just seems like a recipe for disaster."

Monica stared at me for a few seconds, and then we both busted up laughing. I didn't know what she was picturing, but I could imagine me and Bull trying to get busy on his bike only to roll off and crack our heads open or break an arm or something. Then the entire club would know we'd failed at bike sex. We'd never hear the end of it.

Once our laughter died down, Monica asked, "You worried about him icing you out again?"

I thought about it. "No. He told me he loves me, and I believe him. He pushed me away because he was trying to protect me. Now, he knows I'm all in, and that any efforts to thwart me will result in his untimely demise."

"That's my girl." Her proud smile warmed me. Some girls bonded over shopping trips and pedicures. Monica and I bonded over jokes about death threats and stabbing techniques. There wasn't a single person in the world I'd rather have in my corner, and as much as I pretended to hate her prying, I appreciated her nosy-ass self.

"I still can't believe you punched his v-card," Monica said. "I didn't even know there were virgin sailors. Fucked up my entire world view."

"Yeah, it surprised the hell out of me, too. I mean, look at him." I was sure Bull had plenty of offers for sex, but he was a good guy. He'd stayed faithful to Amber even after her death.

"Gotta say, the ex's suicide makes a lot more sense," Monica said. "Can you imagine saving yourself like that and then some asshole rips it all away? She had all these hopes and dreams of this perfect life, and he... he must have shattered her."

Monica could relate. Her Air Force fighter pilot career had been stolen by a sleeping trucker. All her hard work and training gone instantly, her life forever changed. She didn't talk much about the days afterward, but she'd had multiple surgeries that had barely saved her life. Her parents were afraid she was going to give up, so they'd called in Naomi and Stocks. The two of them had kidnapped Monica and brought her to Seattle, where they forced her to remember she was a queen.

"But *you* didn't give up," I pointed out.

"Oh, I wanted to. Trust me. But Naomi... she's a force to be reckoned with. Everyone needs the kind of friend who's unafraid to kick your ass when you need it. Maybe Amber didn't feel like she had that."

That made me sad for the girl. "I still don't understand why she didn't reach out to Bull, but I guess we'll never know."

"Nope." Monica smiled at me. "The only thing we can do now is take care of Bull and make sure none of our own feel that crushing hopelessness alone."

"Deal," I said, smiling back at her.

14

Bull

I SAT ON my bed with an old shoebox in front of me. It had taken me a half hour—and two beers—to work up the courage to remove the lid. Now the contents mocked me, making me feel like a goddamn chicken for wanting to close the box back up and return it to its spot hidden away on the top of my closet.

No. It's time.

Drawing in a ragged breath, I reached for the first item. Amber's last letter, sent just days before her death. I'd received it after I'd gotten out of the brig, and I read it at least a hundred times, searching for clues about her suicide. The folds were worn, making the ink difficult to read in places, but despite not opening the box since I'd arrived in Seattle, I knew the damn thing by heart.

Deryk,

It's been a while since we've connected online, so I wanted to write and check up on you. I miss you, and I'm feeling a little homesick today.

Probably because I've been studying like crazy for finals. I can't wait to go home and rest for the summer, but I wish you were going to be there. It's not the same without you.

James and Molly broke up. She was invited to a party at a frat house and wanted to go. He got upset and they fought. It was super awkward. I swear the entire cafeteria was in on their fight. Molly asked me to go with her to the party, but I don't know. It'd be nice for the whole college experience, but you know me. Frat parties aren't really my thing.

How are you?
Where are you?
I miss you.
I should probably get back to studying. Thank God this year is almost over.
Love always,
Amber

I folded the note back up and set it aside, reaching for the stack of photos and letters beneath it. Our senior prom photo, a picture of us at her cousin's wedding, wrist bands from the county fair, movie tickets from when she dragged my ass to go see *The Fault in Our Stars* with her, so many memories hidden away in a single shoebox. I took out each one and allowed myself to remember the way things really were.

In my memories, Amber and I were both so immature. I thought about the conversations and dreams we'd shared. Like her mother, Amber was a planner. She'd planned out our wedding, the honeymoon, how many kids we'd have, where we'd live, everything. She lived in the future, and painted me a picture of her goals every chance she got. I never questioned her, disagreed, or offered my opinion, choosing to let her rattle on for years about her perfect life. About the life she wanted to share with me.

But looking back now, I realized we didn't dream about the same things.

Amber was planning a big-ass formal wedding, complete with tuxes, gowns, and flowers I couldn't even pronounce. I couldn't care less if our big event was the talk of the town, but she was hung up on the prospect of making it bigger and better than any ceremony before it. I had no desire to live out my days in Shiner, Texas, but she fantasized about a big yellow house, sandwiched between her parents and mine, planning to pop out one kid after the next. Don't get me wrong, I wasn't opposed to having a couple of kids, but Amber had wanted enough to form her own co-ed softball team. I wanted to travel... to adventure. I didn't see how we could go anywhere with a whole herd of kids holding us down.

Still, I let her dream.

Now wondering if I'd always known her dreams would never come to fruition, I pulled every last item from the box. At the bottom, was her ring: a simple princess cut diamond for the girl I believed I'd spend the rest of my life with. I slipped it onto the tip of my index finger and looked it over, expecting the pain of losing her to hit me all over again.

It didn't.

Still sad about her untimely passing, and a little betrayed she hadn't come to me, my heart no longer felt like it was trying to tear itself out of my chest when I thought of her.

It was time to let Amber go. For real, this time.

Scooping up our memories, I stuffed them back in the box and called my parents.

"Hey, Mom." I said when she answered. "How are you?"

"I'm good, Deryk. Better now that you called. It's been too long. We worry when we don't hear from you."

The guilt trips Mom tried to take me on every time I called only made me want to reach out to her less, not more. Besides, my cell worked both ways, and she and Dad hadn't exactly blown up my phone trying to reach me. Hell, I couldn't even remember the last time one of them called. These conversations were awkward for all of us, regardless of how she tried to play them off. Still, there wasn't any way to point that out without sounding like a disrespectful little shit, and I'd been raised better.

"Sorry. You know I don't mean to worry you," I said, accepting the blame. "Is Dad there?"

"He's sitting right here, watching the news. Do you want me to hand him the phone?"

"No. Can you put it on speaker phone so I can talk to you both at the same time?"

"Okay." Mom sounded different, further away.

"You can both hear me?" I asked. When they both confirmed, I sucked down a deep breath and got right to the reason for my call. "I'm seeing someone."

Mom didn't miss a beat. "That's wonderful, Deryk. What's her name?"

"Lily. She's... she's really great."

"What's her family like?" Mom asked.

"She doesn't know where her parents are. Her grandma raised her, but she died a few years ago."

"Oh, that's awful. Poor thing. You should bring her with you for Christmas. We'd love to meet her, wouldn't we, hon?"

"Yeah. Sure," Dad said.

"I don't know if that's such a good idea," I said.

I could hear the news anchor still blabbing in the background, and knew I only had a sliver of my father's attention. Like usual. I had to figure out a way to get his ear so I could adequately explain the situation and make sure they didn't want to rescind Lily's invitation. Opening the drawer of my nightstand, I removed a strip of pictures from the mall photo booth she'd dragged me into during one of our many shopping trips. I always pretended to hate hitting the mall with her, but truthfully, Lily made everything fun. I'd purchased the goofy photos and stashed them in my nightstand, and was damn glad I had. Lily's smiling face had gotten me through a lot of lonely nights and difficult mornings. Using my phone, I snapped a picture of the photo strip and sent it to Mom.

"Why wouldn't it be a good idea, Deryk? Nobody should have to be alone for the holidays," Mom said.

She had me there. Still, I needed Mom to know what we would be dealing with. I could try to explain, but some things were easier shown than told. "I just sent you a picture of Lily."

"You know we don't care what she looks like," Mom huffed. "It's what's on the inside that counts."

I wondered what Mom expected Lily to look like. "It's not like that. She's pretty, Mom. Please… just open the message and look at the picture."

A few seconds later, Mom gasped. "Frank, look," I heard her say. "This girl looks just like Amber. As I live and breathe…"

I heard the television click off.

"That's not Amber?" Dad asked.

"No. That's Lily. She's the lady I'm seeing," I said.

"What is this? Looks just like Bill's girl," Dad sounded upset and confused. "We buried Bill's girl. You remember the funeral, don't you, Liz?"

"Yes. You sure you didn't send us an old picture of you and Amber, honey?" Mom asked.

"Yes. Lily looks a lot like Amber."

"A lot?" Dad snorted. "She's a spittin' image of Bill's girl. The world's a crowded place. How'd you manage to find yourself another Amber?"

My family had loved Amber. I'd expected their acceptance of Lily to be overshadowed by that love, but hearing the accusation in Dad's voice still pissed me off. "I wasn't looking for another Amber. Heck, I wasn't looking for anyone." Knowing I needed to nip this in the bud before they met my woman, I added, "And Lily's nothing like Amber. Yeah, she looks like her, but the two of them couldn't be more different."

"That's too bad. I really liked Amber," Mom said.

Frustrated, I raked a hand through my hair and tried again. "You'd like Lily, too, if you gave her a chance."

"That poor girl. And poor Gretta. Losin' her like she did... it was a cryin' shame."

Mom was getting derailed, and I didn't have it in me to go wandering down memory lane with her. The past had consumed far too much of my time and energy, and I refused to let it draw me in again. I'd made a promise to Lily, and I had every intention of keeping it. "It's been two years, Mom. Don't I deserve to be happy?"

"Yes. Of course, you do, dear. I just... this is kind of shocking."

"I know. If you think it's gonna be too hard on everyone to meet Lily, she and I will stay up here for Christmas."

"But you always come home for Christmas," Mom said.

"Yeah, I do. But like you said, nobody should be alone for the holidays, and I'm not leaving my girl here by herself. That's not the kind of man you raised me to be."

"You won't come if she doesn't?" Mom asked.

"No, ma'am. I know her resemblance to Amber will probably make you and the Kents uncomfortable, but I wouldn't be calling you if I wasn't serious about her. I love Lily. I plan to keep her in my life as long as she'll stay, and I won't bring her down there if she's not welcome."

The silence on the other end of the phone was deafening, confirming every fear I'd had about their reception. They didn't say Lily wasn't welcome, but they didn't have to. It was obvious where they stood on the matter. It hurt like hell, but I'd drawn my line and I wouldn't cross it. I loved my family, but Lily was my future, and they damn well needed to accept her if they ever wanted to see my ass again.

"We have four months until Christmas," I said. "Plenty of time for the two of you to think about it and let me know what you decide."

"Okay." Mom's voice quivered. I wondered if she was still

looking at the pictures of me and Lily. I hoped like hell she didn't still see Amber. "We'll let you know. We love you, Deryk."

"Love you, too." We said our goodbyes and I ended the call and stared at my phone, wondering what my parents would decide. Then I realized I couldn't worry about that right then, because I had shit to do.

Grabbing the shoebox from my bed, I headed downstairs. Naomi and Monica were sitting on one of the sofas discussing something. I stopped by long enough to hand Naomi Amber's ring. She looked from it to me, and her eyebrows rose in question.

"What's this?" she asked.

"A donation for Lady's First. Maybe you can sell it?"

Naomi looked like she wanted to ask a shit-ton more questions, but Monica settled her hand over the ring and smiled at me. "Thank you, Bull. We'll make good use of it."

I was sure they would. Mood lifted, I took my box and headed for the fire pit in the back yard. It was time to let Amber go.

15

Bull

SINCE I HAD the day off, I picked Lily up after work so she wouldn't have to ride the bus. She walked out of the building, talking to an older guy with salt-and-pepper hair, a shaved face, and kind eyes. It had to be Tom, the supervisor who was training Lily. She'd told me all about him, and he seemed like a nice enough guy. Then again, I was pretty sure Lily could find the good in anyone.

As soon as her gaze found me, a smile about split her face in two and she waved wildly. His gaze followed hers, found me, and he frowned. It wasn't the first time someone had seen my cut and my Harley and made a split-second judgment about my character, but it still ruffled my feathers. I wanted to tell him where he could shove his judgment but didn't want to make trouble for Lily at her new job. So, I got off my bike, removed my helmet, and offered the condescending asshole my most disarming smile and my hand.

"Hi. I'm Deryk. Lily's boyfriend."

Lily's smile grew impossibly wider. "Deryk, this is Tom, the super patient supervisor who's been training me."

Tom still didn't look too sure about me, but he shook my hand. His grip was firm, and he looked me in the eye and said, "Nice to meet you."

I turned up the charm. "The pleasure's all mine. Lily has nothing but good things to say about this place. Thank you for taking such good care of her. We're relieved she gets to apprentice in such a positive environment."

His demeanor relaxed marginally. "We're lucky to have her. She's catching on quickly. At this rate, she'll be out in the field in no time."

"Good to hear." Reaching into my back pocket, I pulled out a business card. "I work for a veteran-run and operated tow company. If you ever find yourself in need, please don't hesitate to call."

He turned the card over, and the remaining frost thawed from his demeanor. Apparently my being a veteran trumped my being a biker. Good to know. "Thank you."

Lily beamed Tom a smile. "Thanks again for all your help this week. Have a great weekend."

"You too." He nodded at my bike. "Both of you. Be careful on that thing."

"Yessir." I handed Lily a helmet, letting him see her safety was important to me. "We always are."

Tom headed for his car and Lily put her helmet on, leaning close to say, "Schmooze level, expert. Please teach me your ways, oh great one."

I chuckled. "I can't teach that. That there's my superpower, Angel. I was born with it, but it was honed by Dad's belt and Mom's lectures, which I wouldn't recommend enduring. How was your day?"

"Great, but even better now. I can't believe how much I've missed you this week."

I flipped up her visor and leaned in to give her a quick peck on the lips, completely aware that Tom—and probably others—were watching. One quick taste of her wasn't enough. I wanted to wrap my arms around her and kiss her so long and hard it left no doubt in any motherfucker's mind she was claimed, but I withheld. I'd wait until her job was a little steadier before I started that shit. Instead, I put my helmet back on, mounted my bike, and offered her my hand. Lily slid on behind me, wrapping herself around my core.

It wasn't the first time we rode together.

No, Lily had been on the back of my bike more times than I could count. To some bikers, the back of a bike is sacred, used only for long-term relationship women. But, outside of my work truck, I only had one form of transportation. I wasn't going to make Lily walk, so she was often at my back. But now that our relationship had evolved, her presence felt different. Everywhere our bodies touched felt like a promise of more to come... more heat, more comfort, more intimacy.

Enjoying the feel of her behind me, I was tempted to take the long way to the shelter, but it had been almost a full week since I'd had her writhing beneath me, and was desperate to repeat the experience. Just thinking about all the ways I wanted to fuck her had me riding the throttle like a sinner busting out of hell.

We made a quick pit stop to feed Brahma and let him out, and found Stocks placing decorative rocks around a tree trunk. He stopped what he was doing and wandered over to join us.

"Hey brother. Lily," he said with a wave. "You two off to the fire station?"

"Yep. You'll be there for church tonight, right?"

"Yeah. I'll see you there." Stocks's gaze followed Brahma. "You know, Lil, you don't have to come home tonight if you don't want to. I can let Brahma out and make sure he gets fed in the morning."

Hope filled her eyes as she looked to me, and then to Stocks. "But he's my responsibility, and I don't want to inconvenience anyone."

"Please. He's the most mellow dog I've ever met. He'll be fine.

Taming Bull

Go. Enjoy yourself. Remember you're in your mid-twenties and have a fuckin' weekend for once. I've got the mutt."

Lily dropped the pooper scooper and plastic bags to jump down and hug Stocks. "You're the best adoptive dad, big brother, security guard, maintenance man, best friend's husband ever. Thank you."

He chuckled. "Yeah, yeah. I'm the shit."

She laughed. "Yes. You are definitely the shit."

She reached for the pooper scooper, but I stopped her. "Go pack. I'll clean up after Brahma."

Bouncing on her heels, she gave me a hug too. "Fine, you can be the shit, too." Before I could respond, she went bounding into the house.

"Thanks, brother," I told Stocks.

He leveled a stare at me. "I know I don't have to tell you this, but Lily means a lot to all of us. What are your intentions with her?"

It felt somewhat surreal to have the question lobbed at me by someone who wasn't even a full decade older than me, but I appreciated the way he and Monica took Lily under their wings and looked out for her. I rocked back on my heels and thought about where I wanted this thing with Lily to go. "We haven't really defined the relationship, but we're exclusive. I love her, and I'm all in. I'm not gonna do anything to hurt her."

He nodded and clapped me on the shoulder. "Good. See that you don't. If I have to bail Monica out of jail for killin' your ass, I'll dig you up and kill you again. Got it?"

I chuckled. "Loud and clear."

"Great. My job here is done."

He went back to his rocks, and I picked up dog shit until Lily was ready to go. She'd changed out of her work clothes and into a pair of distressed skinny jeans, boots, and a tight black tank top. She swung her backpack over her shoulder and nodded toward the door. I glanced at Brahma, wondering if we should get the dog inside before we left.

"Leave him," Stocks said, reading my mind. "I can use the company."

He didn't have to tell us twice. Excited to be spending some real quality time with her, I grabbed Lily's hand and towed her toward my bike. We made it back to the fire station in record time. There were a handful of people milling about in the common area, so we sneaked in the back entrance like a couple of teenagers hoping to get lucky. It wasn't that we didn't want anyone to know what we were up to, we just wanted to be alone. Sneaking around with her was surprisingly hot, and by the time we made it to my room, I was so wound up, it was all I could do to keep myself from ripping her clothes off. Locking the door behind us, I spun her around, putting her back to the wood. Her eyes were wild and her cheeks were rosy as she giggled.

"I don't think anyone saw us," she breathed.

Whisps of hair had escaped from her braid to frame her face. I tucked them behind her ears, letting my fingers linger on her jaw. "You're so fuckin' beautiful, Angel."

Heat flooded her eyes. Our mouths mashed together and our tongues danced, getting reacquainted after what felt like forever. She wrapped her legs around my waist, and I trapped her between my body and the door as I explored her mouth with my tongue. The heat of her core against me teased and tempted, ramping everything up.

Breaking apart, she tugged her tank top over her head and tossed it aside before grabbing at the hem of my shirt. I removed it. The satiny fabric of her bra felt good, but not nearly as good as her skin. Reaching around her, I unfastened her bra and slid it over her arms before pressing against her. Much better. The door shuddered under our combined weight, bouncing off the frame. Lily moaned, and the sound went straight to my cock.

"More. I need you inside me," she said, reaching between us to fumble with the button of my jeans.

Thank fuck.

Needing her every bit as much as she needed me, I set her down and unfastened my pants, letting them fall to my ankles. Since I didn't work today, and knew I'd be picking up Lily, I hadn't bothered with boxers. Her eyes rounded, doing wonders for my self-esteem, as her hand landed on my shaft. She kicked off her boots. While her soft, small hands tugged on me, I removed her pants and thong before running my fingers through her slick folds.

"So fucking soaked for me," I said.

She nodded. "Yes. I want you bad."

This time she wrapped her legs back around my waist, I lined myself up with her entrance and sunk into her wet heat. She took every inch of me, her tight channel spreading to accept my girth. Her pebbled nipples called to me. Dipping my head, I sucked one into my mouth as I played with the other. Lily moaned. Her head fell back, hitting the door.

"Ouch." She rubbed at it.

I froze, afraid to injure her further. "You okay?"

"Yes. Don't stop." She squeezed my cock inside her, and I almost blacked out.

My breaths came out ragged as I caged her between myself and the wood, driving into her again and again. Each time the door bounced against the frame, knocking. By now, everyone knew we were together, but I respected Lily too much to announce that we were fucking. Some things should remain private. Pulling her away from the door, I kept us joined as I waddled across the room.

When we reached the sofa, she released me and climbed down, bending over the cloth arm. I took a minute to admire her fine heart-shaped ass and appreciate the fact she was all mine.

Mine.

The claim resonated within me. No matter what, this girl was mine, and I refused to give her up.

Looking over her shoulder, she gave me a knowing smirk. "You just gonna look at me all day?"

"Thinkin' about it. You do look damn good."

But my cock was throbbing, wanting more of her. I lined myself back up, grabbed her hips, and plowed into her. She grunted and dropped her head to the seat cushion.

"Yes. Right there. Oh, God."

Her building pleasure inspired my own. Heat sprouted at my backbone and spread through my entire body. Having her bent over like this... positioned especially for my pleasure... it was goddamn perfect. Every time I sheathed myself into her tight, slick pussy, I was in danger of busting a nut. Both nuts. Hell, I was surprised my entire body didn't explode. Watching myself slide in and out of her hot channel was erotic as fuck. Knowing I was hanging on by a thread and needed to get her on my level, I wrapped one hand around her and started circling her clit as I continued to fuck her.

"Get there, Lily," I ordered. I was close and didn't want to come without her.

"Oh God, that feels so good," she said, arching her back to take me in deeper.

My hand continued to work her clit as I fucked her. Within minutes, we were both tumbling over the edge in a sweaty, sated mess.

I pushed her French braid aside to kiss her neck. "Mine," I whispered, enjoying the resulting goosebumps that sprouted across her flesh.

16

Lily

THE PARK WAS bustling with activity when Brahma and I arrived Sunday afternoon. Sun shining, temperature in the low eighties, it was the perfect combination to draw every kid in the neighborhood between ages two and ten. The energetic little psychos ran back and forth from the dog park to the play structure in some bizarre game of tag with rules I was clearly too old to understand. Regardless, the entire group had come to the consensus that a little boy named Dylan was cheating and they wanted him to stop. They kept yelling it over and over.

Johnny saw me and Brahma approach and peeled off from the group to join us, tackling the dog in a hug.

"What's going on here?" I asked, eyeing the rambunctious kids.

Johnny pointed at a brown-skinned child in the middle of the group who had the frustrated expression of someone trying to herd cats or decode instructions in a foreign language. I couldn't help but feel bad for him. "That's Oscar. He just joined a flag football team, so he's trying to teach us the rules." He pointed to another little boy. "That's Dylan. He says it's Opposite Day and we need to do the opposite of whatever Oscar says."

Chaos. Complete and total pandemonium. I'd known Dylans in my lifetime, and they all needed a swift kick in the ass. "If you want to keep playing with Oscar, you can. BB and I are gonna be here for a while."

"No. Oscar's okay, but Dylan's kind of a bully, and I would much rather spend time with BB. Huh, boy?" Johnny pulled a ball out of his pocket.

Brahma did his best not to roll his eyes at me before dutifully running after the ball. Call me crazy, but I didn't think fetch was his favorite game.

Parents loomed along the sidelines and chatted as their spawns raced back, screaming about cheaters, in their sabotaged game of flag football. Finding Shelly, I sidled up to her and asked how she was doing.

"Good. Much better than Tina over there." She nodded toward a woman with streaked mascara running down her face. "Apparently her husband lost his temper yesterday and she had to file a restraining order against him." Shelly shook her head. "Poor woman. I thought John was bad, but at least the cheating bastard never laid a hand on me or Johnny. I probably would have snapped, killed him, and ended up in jail. You know it's a horrible state of affairs when I feel lucky my husband was *just* a cheater."

"Men can be assholes," I agreed. "But there are good ones out there."

She didn't look so sure. "I'll have to take your word for it. I have no intention of going down that road again any time soon."

I almost offered to introduce her to some hot, single veterans, but it was too soon. Shelly needed time to heal before she even thought about diving into another relationship. It had taken Bull more than two years. I was hoping it wouldn't take her nearly as long because she was a good person who shouldn't have to be lonely.

Every time Bull so much as crossed my mind, I felt twitterpated, like I was in some sweet Disney movie, dancing among the wildlife as I made plans for the perfect future with the man of my dreams. Monica had ratted him out for donating an engagement ring—a ring that had to be Amber's—to Ladies First. She'd sent me a picture and everything. Seeing the ring he'd intended to marry another woman with was difficult, but the knowledge that he'd donated it helped wipe the tears from my eyes. My man was finally moving on, and he was doing so *with* me. His progress was huge, and I was so damn excited I could hardly sit still.

Thinking of Ladies First had me eyeing Tina. Monica had stocked me with the group's business cards with situations like this in mind. I didn't know Tina from Eve, and there was something seriously fucked up about me inviting myself into her business. The idea of walking over and striking up a conversation about a stranger's abusive ex didn't appeal to me at all. But, I had resources that could possibly offer the help she needed. Others had helped me, and it would be a dick move not to return the favor.

Karma seemed to finally be on my side, and I wasn't about to fuck that up.

Gathering my courage, I pulled a business card from my backpack and marched toward Tina. She had friends on either side of her, making me rethink my interference. Clearly, she had people. I bet she had this shit covered and didn't need my resources at all. Still, I was already on the move, so I might as well connect. Worst case scenario, she'd tell me to mind my own business, and I'd avoid her anytime I came to the park. Or maybe we'd find a different park to meet Shelly and Johnny at.

When I was halfway to Tina, she looked up at me. Her eyes widened with fear.

I froze wondering why the hell she was looking at me like that.

She bolted to her feet. "No, Matt! Someone stop him! He has Dylan!"

Oh. She was looking behind me to where the kids were

running. I spun around to see a dark-haired man in his later thirties who had Dylan the bully wrapped in his arms. He was tugging the boy away from the field as Dylan flailed his arms and legs, trying to get away.

"Mom!" Dylan shouted.

I was the closest adult to them.

There was no time to think shit through. My legs automatically started running on their own, closing the distance between me and Dylan. All that sprinting practice finally proved useful as I dashed across the field at my top speed. I don't know how many other adults were at my back—if any—but Matt looked up, saw me, and doubled his efforts. Dylan went crazy, and Matt backhanded him. The kid's eyes widened as shock and anger restricted his movements.

Matt kept backpedaling, but I was gaining on him. My legs and chest burned, but adrenaline and momentum carried me. Dylan saw me and ducked. I lunged at Matt, and he released the kid. Our bodies crashed together in a loud thwack. Pain registered, sending fire up my left side. Dylan rolled to the side. Matt went down with me on top of him. He grunted as the air was knocked out of him.

Holding still, I took stock of my aching body. I was sore, but nothing felt broken. My ears rang. In the background, I could hear one of the parents shouting something about the police being on their way.

"What the fuck are you doing?" Matt asked, his hands wrapped around my throat. "I'm gonna fuckin' kill you, you interfering little bi—" The word was cute off with a blood curling scream.

Matt's grip relaxed. I moved out of his strangling range and found Brahma, his teeth locked around the bastard's jean-clad leg. Shocked, it took me a minute to register what I was seeing. I hadn't seen my dog run, nor had I heard him bark or let out any sort of warning before he attacked. He'd seen that I was in danger, and reacted. Matt tried to kick his leg free, but Brahma growled and doubled down. My sweet, borderline lethargic rescue mutt was a vicious guard dog after all.

Who knew?

"Good boy," I crooned.

"Good boy?" Matt spat. "Fuckin' beast is eating my goddamn leg! Get him the fuck off me!"

Matt was still a flight risk who needed to be brought to justice, but parents were surrounding us in a concerned circle. Figuring nobody would let the bastard get far, I said, "Let him go, Brahma."

The dog looked at me.

"Release?" I tried.

He unlocked his jaw and took a step back, sitting like he was awaiting further instruction. Regardless of what happened here today, I planned to give him all the dog treats his round little belly could handle. He'd earned them.

"Good boy, Brahma," I said again.

Matt looked at me like I'd lost my mind. "He's not a good boy! He fuckin' bit me."

Kids were joining us now. One gasped at his dropping of the F-bomb.

"Language," a parent chided.

Matt flipped off the parent and shoved me away. "Get off me so I can at least see how bad the wound is."

I sat back on my heels as he doubled over to yank up the leg of his jeans. The bite marks were bleeding, but they didn't look deep enough for stitches.

"Look at this!" he shouted. "I'm gonna sue your ass and have that mutt put to sleep."

"Like hell you will," one dad said. "Plenty of witnesses here who saw you try to kidnap that kid."

"My son," Matt corrected.

"Restraining order," Tina countered.

"Oh, come on," I groaned, looking over his leg. "I've hurt myself worse biking, you big baby. Maybe you shouldn't lay hands on your wife if you don't want my dog sinking his teeth in your leg, a-hole."

A few of the parents snickered and I mentally patted myself on the back for throwing out the zinger.

The cops arrived and busted up our little party, asking questions and taking statements. Tina thanked me and patted Brahma on the head. I handed her the business card I'd been walking over to give her, and she promised to give Ladies First a call.

Matt demanded an ambulance, but one of the officers treated his leg, rolled his eyes, and stuffed the blabbering wimp into the back of the police cruiser instead.

An officer took me and Brahma to the shelter and waited as I retrieved Brahma's shot records to prove he didn't have rabies or any other contagious diseases. The officer took a picture of the shot records and my ID, went over my statement again, and told me not to leave town for a while in case they needed me to testify. As the cop was pulling away, Bull arrived.

He parked, ripped off his helmet, and looked me over, his expression full of concern. "What the fuck's goin' on? Everything okay?"

Happy to see him, I hurried over and gave him a kiss. "Yep. Just me and Brahma being heroes and shit."

His eyebrows rose in question. "You're not hurt or in trouble?"

"No. I told you, we saved the day. Come on in, I'll tell you all about it," I said.

"Actually, I was hoping you'd come with me." He held out the second helmet. "I have a surprise to show you."

My heart kicked up as I eyed him. "What is it?"

His expression told me nothing. "I told you, a surprise."

He knew I lived for surprises. "Will I like this surprise?" I asked.

He shrugged, a smirk tugging at his lips. "Only one way to find out."

Excited, I tried not to squeal in delight as I herded Brahma into the house and gave him a couple of treats with the promise of more. Then I hopped on the back of Bull's bike and put on my helmet.

Instead of heading for the freeway, we drove a handful of blocks deeper into the neighborhood, coming to a stop in front of a little gray bungalow. Bull parked, offered me his arm, and dismounted behind me. Removing my helmet, I shook out my hair and looked around. I could feel his gaze on me as I took in the wooden "For Sale" real estate sign with "Pending" clipped beneath it. Thick bushes lined the sidewalk and the sides of the house. A concrete driveway led to an attached garage, and a concrete walkway led to a freshly painted red front door that looked inviting.

Bull linked his arm in mine and tugged me forward. "Come on."

"Where are we?" I asked.

Before he could answer, the red door swung open and a bubbly blonde in her mid-thirties stepped out to greet us. "Hello, Deryk, good to see you again."

"Jenna." He nodded. "This is my girlfriend, Lily." To me, he added, "Jenna's my real estate agent."

Bull had a real estate agent? Confused, I shook the hand she offered and tried to sort through the scraps of information I'd collected.

Jenna walked back into the house, and Bull nudged me to follow her. We stepped into a living room. The stark white walls held a few nails and looked like they could use a good washing and a coat of paint. The carpet beneath my feet had seen better days as well. I couldn't see much past the two archways leading out of the living room, but the place smelled clean, and it was bright and airy.

"Do you have any questions?" Jenna asked.

I had so many, but she wasn't talking to me.

"What happens now?" Bull asked.

She went through the archway at the back of the room to the left, leading us through a square dining room and turning right toward a small kitchen. Stopping at the bar that separated the two rooms, she pulled her briefcase over her shoulder and started thumbing through it. "Now that your offer's been accepted, I just have a few more forms for you to sign, and then we're looking at closing mid-September. I'll let you know the exact date once we hear back from your lender." She set a manilla folder on the bar and opened it. "I've marked all the places you need to sign with sticky notes."

"Thank you," Bull said, glancing at the folder. "Do you mind if I show Lily around the place first?"

"Not at all." Jenna glanced at her cell phone. "In fact, I need to step out and make a call. Just leave the folder on the bar when you're finished, and I'll grab it before I lock up and head out."

I watched her go back the way we came before spinning on my heel to face Bull. "You bought a house?"

"Yeah. You want to see the rest of it?"

"Are you kidding me? Of course, I want to see it. I can't believe you didn't tell me!"

He chuckled. "Didn't want to get our hopes up until they accepted the offer. I know it's not much to look at, but Spade said it has good bones and everything it needs is cosmetic. Won't take much to fix it up. The roof is only a couple years old, and all the plumbing and electrical was rewired in the late nineties." Bull led me into the small kitchen. The cabinets and laminate floor were dated, but the large window over the sink opened the space up, making it bright and welcoming.

"We'll need to shop for a stove and refrigerator. A couple of bar stools. Spade's giving me a stellar discount on new cupboards and granite countertops. Said he'll even help with the install. Good thing, since I have no clue what I'm doing. Stocks offered his services too. I can't tell you how lucky we are to have knowledgeable friends who aren't afraid to roll up their sleeves and help."

My cheeks were burning from smiling so hard. "I still can't believe you bought a house."

"Crazy, huh?" He grinned. "The flooring is all shit. I figured we can install hardwood." He led me through the dining area to a small laundry room. "Maybe tile in here. We'll need to buy a washer and dryer, too. Maybe a stackable set, since the space is kind of tight and it's just the two of us."

The way he kept including me in his plans made my chest swell and my smile grow impossibly wider. I was so damn happy it was all I could do to keep from bursting at the seams.

"The walls can use a coat of paint, but I figured we'll do that once we know what we want to do with the floors. Then we can color coordinate and shit."

He led me back through the living room and around to open the door to a small coat closet. Another door led to the bathroom. Like everything else, it was small, but it did have a clean tub and shower combo, a toilet, and a sink. The windows over the shower let in a lot of natural light, which seemed to be the theme of the house.

"Tile in here, too," Bull said, frowning at the worn, dated vinyl flooring before leading me into a small bedroom. "I was thinking new carpet for the bedrooms, but maybe it'd be best if we put wood down in here, too. Then we can use some throw rugs to cozy it up. Maybe put a little desk and chair in here, and you can use it to study when you have to test again."

I didn't know what to say, so I followed him into the slightly larger bedroom across the way.

"This is the master. The closet's kinda small, but neither one of us have many clothes, so I think it'll work just fine. I can always use the closet in the spare bedroom if we run out of space. We'll need to shop for furniture." Bull's eyes lit up. "Not gonna lie, I'm looking forward to picking out a bed with you. Probably can't fit a king in here, but a queen would do nicely."

All his plans for his new house included me. Emotions choked me and kept trying to leak out of my eyes.

"Come on, let me show you the rest of it." Bull sounded somewhat disappointed as he gave me a quick tour of the garage before leading me through the sliding glass doors in the kitchen. We stood on a raised wooden deck that needed to be stained and sealed, and looked over a weed-filled yard surrounded by a tall wooden fence. The space would be perfect for Brahma.

Tears I could no longer blink back, streamed down my cheeks.

Concern clouded Bull's eyes as he wiped them away. "I know it's not much, but there weren't many options in my price range that had space for a dog. It's close to the shelter and the fire station, and if we put in the work, we can sell this place for twice what I bought it for and find someplace better. In the meantime, we'll be able to stay together. I'll be able to spend every night with you, without having to worry about getting you home so you can take care of the dog and get some sleep."

Realizing he must have misinterpreted my tears, I shook my head. "Bull, it's perfect. Ohmigod, I love it so much! These aren't tears of sadness. I'm so happy I could..." I wrapped my arms around him and squeezed tight. "I don't even know what to say. You didn't officially ask me, but you bet your ass I'm moving in here with you. I'm still floored you bought a house. In Seattle, even. How can you afford this?"

"My grandparents set up trust funds for me and my sister when we were little. They grew up poor and struggled to do shit like buy a house until Grandpa's business took off. They've been sittin' pretty for years and wanted to pass along their good fortune. Or that's the story they gave me. I'm financing some of the loan so we have money for shit like furniture, appliances, and repairs, but I can easily handle the payment with what I make while saving money for us to travel."

"And I'll help," I said.

"You're still apprenticing. You can buy groceries and stuff if you want, but I got this." He cupped my face in his hands. "I want to do this for you. For us. And for that useless mutt of yours."

Offended, I poked him in the chest with my index finger. "I'll have you know my mutt is not useless. He helped me take down a would-be kidnapper at the park today. That's why the cop was there. I tackled the guy, and Brahma bit his leg."

Bull stared at me skeptically. "You're shittin' me."

"I most certainly am not. I told you he was protective."

Shaking his head, Bull chuckled. "Well, I'll be. I guess it's a good thing we'll have the beast around guarding the place."

"He'll love it here. This is so perfect, babe," I said, leaning into Bull as he wrapped his arms around me. "We'll have privacy! I can't wait to christen every room in the house."

His eyes darkened. "That's definitely a benefit to having our own place."

He dropped his lips to mine in a sweet, gentle kiss full of promises and hopes. Then I led him into the kitchen to sign the last of the paperwork. We had plans to make and shopping to do, and more than anything, we needed to get back to the fire station so I could show my man exactly how excited I was about our new home.

EPILOGUE

Bull

"DON'T BE NERVOUS," I whispered to Lily before knocking on the door. It was my childhood home and I technically didn't have to knock, but barging into my parents' home felt invasive to me. Even if they were expecting us.

"How?" Lily asked, rubbing her sweaty palms on her jeans.

She'd purchased a long skirt and flowery blouse she described as "wholesome church girl style" that she had wanted to wear for my parents, but she looked completely different in them. I didn't want her buying new shit to impress my folks, so I had her return the outfit. Lily was perfect as she was, and she didn't need to change for anyone. Instead, she wore the same distressed skinny jeans, boots, and sweater she'd wear if we were back home. She had kept her makeup light, and left her long brown hair down, making her look soft and casual.

Personally, I preferred my woman with no makeup and no clothes, hair mussed, spread out before me like a fucking buffet. I'd had a lot of time to enjoy that look on her in the months since we'd moved into our little house, but I couldn't get enough of it. Or of her, for that matter.

"How what?" I asked, realizing she'd asked me a question I had yet to answer.

"How do I *not* be nervous? These are your parents. I need to make a good first impression, and you wouldn't let me wear the innocent clothes."

I shook my head at her. "You don't need them, Angel. I told you, I'm so fuckin' impressed with you, I don't give a shit what anyone else thinks."

Her eyes softened. "I love you."

Knocking again, I slid my hand into hers. "I love you, too. I got you. It'll be fine, no matter what."

My parents answered and after the stunned second they took to process Lily's resemblance to Amber in person, they hugged us and welcomed us into their home. As usual, Christmas decorations were everywhere. An enormous, professionally decorated Douglass Fir brushed against the high ceiling of the living room, looking a far cry nicer than the sparse wannabe Charlie Brown tree Lily and I had back home.

"Your home is gorgeous," Lily said to Mom as she took it all in. A life-size nutcracker stood guard by a table with a Christmas village. The place smelled of cinnamon, apples, and Christmas.

"Thank you, dear," Mom replied, smiling as she patted Lily on the hand. "It's a bit much, but I do love to decorate for the holidays."

We slipped through the living room, following boughs of holly into the family room where Grandpa and Grandma were deep in a competitive game of gin rummy against my sister and her husband. Everyone but my sister stood when we entered.

"Mom, Dad, Marilynn, Fred," Dad said, scooting by us. "This is Lily, Deryk's girlfriend."

The welcoming smiles and greetings of my grandparents, sister, and brother-in-law helped ease more of the tension from Lily.

"You can call us Grandma and Grandpa," Grandma said, gesturing Lily forward. "Everyone does."

"Thank you." Lily stepped into Grandma's embrace before accepting a hug from Grandpa, too.

"And this little ball of fuss is Madison," Marilynn said, raising her cards so we could see the baby sleeping on her lap. "I'm not gonna get up because I just got her to sleep, but it's so nice to finally meet you, Lily."

"Thank you. You, as well. And Madison is adorable," Lily gushed.

My sister smiled and brushed back her baby's thick hair. "Yes, she is. I think we'll keep her."

"Hey Fred," I said with a nod.

"Deryk." He nodded back. My brother-in-law was an all right guy, but we'd never had much in common to talk about.

Everyone sat. I positioned Lily beside me on the chaise lounge as Mom and Dad took up their position on the love seat across the coffee table from Grandma and Grandpa. Marilynn and Fred were opposite me and Lily, on the other side of the sectional.

Mom picked up her cards. "I trust nobody cheated while we were gone," she said, eyeing the room. It was the same look she used to give me and Marilynn when she knew we'd filched treats but couldn't prove our guilt.

"Mom, please," Marilynn said, looking up from her cards. "Give us some credit." She winked at Grandma, and Grandma winked back.

Mom rolled her eyes at them. "Jesus doesn't like cheats and liars."

"Then I think you have some repenting to do after that last game," Grandpa said.

Mom harrumphed and everyone else laughed.

Lily sat quietly and took it all in. As Grandpa's turn came and went, she leaned closer to me and whispered, "Do they really cheat?"

I chuckled. "Every one of them... every chance they get."

"Boy, don't you be tellin' stories about us," Grandma said. "Don't you go poisoning that girl before she gets a chance to know us." To Lily, Grandma added, "Don't let him fool you. You're sittin' with the biggest cheat of all."

Lily gasped. "*You* cheat?" she asked me. "Against your grandma?"

Grandma laughed. "He sure does." To Mom, she added, "I like her, Liz. She's adequately appalled by your son's behavior."

Lily was still staring at me in opened-mouth horror.

I held up my hands, trying to ward off her judgement. "Hey, Grandma's ruthless. I gotta win sometimes."

I was afraid there'd be tension and awkwardness, but my family's competitive shenanigans had Lily fully relaxed and laughing in no time. She helped Mom and Grandma bring out the food and held Madison while Marilynn ate. She even got into a heated debate with my dad about why the Seahawks were better than the Cowboys, and held her own against Grandpa's signature teasing.

Watching her interact with them all, I realized Lily had never had this. Sure, she'd grown up with her grandmother, and now she had the club, but she'd never had a family Christmas dinner that ended in a high stakes Scrabble match that required a dictionary, a rosary, and a swear jar. My mom had put up a stocking for Lily, and when Lily saw it, she started bawling.

As Mom draped her arm over Lily's shoulder and took her for a walk to talk, I knew everything was going to be okay. Lily needed this. I hadn't trusted my family to welcome her, but man had they ever proven me wrong.

Since we weren't married, Mom put us up in separate rooms. I sneaked into Lily's room in the middle of the night, and she reluctantly gave me a chaste kiss before chasing my ass out.

"I'm not spitting in the face of your parents' hospitality," she told me.

I couldn't have loved her more if I tried.

Dad asked when I was planning to marry her. I told him we were in no hurry and wanted to travel and see some of the world before we blew money on a wedding. He offered to pick up the tab for our ceremony, but I declined. I appreciated his generosity, but some things we needed to do for ourselves. When we were ready to get married, we'd pay for it on our own. But for now, our plates were full, and our love was enough. We didn't need a piece of paper to make it official.

We returned to Seattle to spend New Year's Eve with the club. While we were away, a new recruit had joined. Link introduced him to me as Kaos, which was apparently his nickname when he played hockey.

"Hockey?" I asked, certain I must have misheard him. "Professionally?"

Kaos nodded. He was a big man. Standing at least six-three, two hundred and fifty pounds of muscle with broad shoulders and a shit-eating grin, he just looked like trouble. "NHL. Played center for the Sharks before I enlisted."

I knew very little about hockey and made a mental note to look up the position and find out what the hell he did. "Holy shit. You were pro and you enlisted?"

He shrugged. "I was getting old. Didn't know what else to do."

He was maybe forty, but I supposed that was old for a hockey player. "And now you're prospecting?"

"Yep. The prez said you can show me around and take me out on the tow truck. He said if I like it and I'm interested, there's openings for drivers. I'll just need to get certified." I briefly wondered why Link kept pushing the new guys off onto me. Tavonte had turned out to be pretty fucking cool, so hopefully this crazy hockey player would, too.

"And you're thinking about it?"

"Sure. Why not?"

This was the most bizarre conversation I'd had in a while. I wanted to point out that he was an NHL player and should be set for life. He'd ben a professional athlete, for crying out loud. Curious about his motivation for wanting to slum with us lowly working-class citizens, I asked, "Did you gamble away all your money or something?"

He glared at me. "What the fuck's that supposed to mean? You think just because I want to work, I must be broke? You think hockey players are too stupid to keep from blowing their money?" He stood, flexing as his hands formed fists.

Wow. He'd read way into my harmless question, and judging by the steam coming out of his ears, he was pissed. "No, man, I didn't mean any of that. I just... I've never met a professional athlete before and—"

He pressed his lips together. I was afraid for my life, so it took me a minute to realize he was trying not to laugh. The corded muscle along his arms relaxed, and he belted out a deep, loud chuckle. "I'm just fuckin' with you, brother." He took a swig from his beer and added, "You gotta learn to relax."

I was pretty sure my life flashed before my eyes, but okay. Yeah. I could relax. Kaos. Now I understood where he got his nickname. I bet he was anarchy and pandemonium on the ice and the battlefield. Ah well. If the bastard fucked with me again, I'd drop his ass off at Ms. Moore's house. At about half her age with muscles to spare, she'd love him. That'd teach the motherfucker.

"I'm lookin' forward to working with you, Kaos," I told him.

He chuckled again. "Sure you are."

Across the room, Lily yawned. She saw me watching and gave me a reassuring smile. She was tired, and although I appreciated my brothers, I had no desire to be in the club when the ball dropped. I collected my woman and we said our goodbyes before heading home.

Parking in the garage beside the used Honda Civic Rabbit had fixed up for Lily, I sent Lily inside before retrieving the gift I'd been working on from its hiding spot under my workbench. I'd wrapped it last night, so I stuck a bow to the top and carried it into the house.

We'd done a lot of work over the past few months, painting, installing new floors, redoing the trim, and updating the light fixtures. There was still more to do, but we enjoyed working together and were in no hurry to finish it. The place was a work in progress... kind of like us.

I removed my boots and went to find Lily. Brahma was sprawled out across his bed in the living room. He opened an eye, saw it was me, and went back to sleep. I still hadn't seen one ounce of the protective guard dog Lily claimed he was, but we did have a copy of a police report that said he'd bit some guy named Matt Warner. Matt was still in jail, doing time for breaking a restraining order and attempted kidnapping. According to Lily, Matt's ex-wife, Tina, and their badass little son were working with Ladies First and doing great.

I found Lily in the bathroom. She'd stripped down to a sheer red nightgown that barely covered her ass, and was brushing her teeth. I took one look at her and my cock turned to granite.

"You look nice," I said, closing in to kiss her cheek.

She spit and rinsed her brush, eyeing the large, heavy package in my hands. "Thanks. What do you have there?"

"It's a surprise."

She worried her bottom lip. "Were we supposed to get New Year's gifts for each other?"

"Nope. This isn't for New Year's."

Putting her toothbrush away, she followed me into the bedroom. "What's it for then?"

"It's because I love you and I wanted to make you something special."

She eyed me. "You said you don't make things."

"Okay. I wanted to buy you something special and refinish it."

She grinned.

I put the package on the bed and watched her expectantly. When she didn't move, I asked, "You gonna open it?"

Lily fell on it and shredded the paper. I laughed, watching her face light up as she realized what it was. "A hope chest?" she asked, lifting the lid.

Made of old cedar, it had been in horrible shape when I'd purchased it, but I'd sanded it down and added protective metal strips to give it that steampunk look she was so fond of.

"Yep. I figured you'd need something to pack all your memories into since we're about to start traveling."

"We are?" she asked, her hands clapping together in excitement.

"Yep. Tay invited us to Nashville. You interested?"

"Ohmigod, yes!" Lily squealed. "You are so getting the best blow job of your life tonight."

I laughed. "Deal. Goddamn, I'll take that deal any day of the week."

"Thank you for this. It's gorgeous, and I can't wait to fill it." She started to move the hope chest, but it was heavy, so I lifted it for her, settling it at the end of our bed.

As soon as my hands were empty, Lily slid between them, tugging off my cut and shirt and removing my jeans and boxers. Her hands roamed over the ridges of my muscles, admiringly, and I made a mental note to keep hitting the gym. I needed to stay in shape for my woman, after all.

"Tell me about this blow job you intend to give me," I said. "I need to be prepared."

She led me to the side of the bed, and then dropped to her knees on the throw rug. "Well." She licked precum from the head of my cock and I groaned. "Considering you're such a giving, caring boyfriend, I think I should try to suck your soul out through your cock."

Could be painful, could be bliss, but I was down. "Show me."

Smiling up at me, she slid my cock between her lips and started sucking. As the clock struck midnight, bringing in a new year, I watched in awe as Lily tried her damnedest to swallow me whole. Lily often joked about her struggle from the friend zone I'd tried to keep her locked away in. I was beyond grateful my angel had found a way to break out of it and wake my ass up.

I didn't know if she could suck my soul out, but she sure as hell had captured my fucking heart.

ALSO BY HARLEY STONE

Thank you so much for reading **Taming Bull**. I hope you've enjoyed the journey. Please take a moment to write a review. They only require twenty words and help me tremendously. I appreciate your support!

Also, be sure to check out my other books:

Link'd Up: Dead Presidents MC #1

Wreaking Havoc: Dead Presidents MC #2

Trapping Wasp: Dead Presidents MC #3

Landing Eagle: Dead Presidents MC #4

Tap'd Out: Dead Presidents MC #5

Breaking Spade: Dead Presidents MC #6

Betting on Stocks: Dead Presidents MC #7

Unleashing Hound: Dead Presidents MC #8

Rescuing Mercy: Dead Presidents MC Spin-off

Dom's Ascension: Mariani Crime Family #1

Making Angel: Mariani Crime Family #2

Breaking Bones: Mariani Crime Family #3

ABOUT THE AUTHOR

International bestselling author Harley Stone is a lover of animals, books, dark chocolate, and red wine. She's always up for a good adventure (real or fictional), and when she's not building imaginary worlds, she's dipping her toes into reality in southwest Washington with her husband and their boys.

ACKNOWLEDGMENTS

This book would have never become a reality without the help and support of so many people. Special thanks to my husband, Meltarrus, our boys, and all my friends and family for letting me off the hook when I daydreamed storyline and dialog during our conversations.

Huge thanks to the incredible Gail Goldie, who saw this first and saved the rest of the world from having to read most of my mistakes. Also, thanks to my fabulous friend Nicole Phoenix for her content edits, suggestions, and encouragement. Thank you, beta and ARC readers for your edits, support, and love.

And, thank you, reader, for embarking on this journey with me!

Printed in Great Britain
by Amazon